UNFINISHED BUSINESS

ROXANNE HENSLEY

For my mother, Linda, a truly amazing woman.

1

Adrian Foley looked in the mirror, vigorously scrubbing her hands until they turned red. A pounding pulse thudded in her ears. She needed to hold it together, at least for the duration of her next meeting, which started in five minutes. She focused on breathing steadily, trying to calm her nerves.

In, out, in, out.

She'd gotten her period. Again. How could her body continuously betray her? Adrian had done her research. She'd read all the blogs and advice she could find. She'd even kept track of her basal temperatures throughout the month and used an in-home ovulation kit as a supposedly foolproof backup plan. She was determined to get it right.

And they'd consummated several times during her monthly peak, to the point where Brad said he felt worn out. She couldn't fail. Yet, once again, her pesky Aunt Flo came to visit.

Adrian fought back tears as she gripped the counter with damp hands, staring at herself in the mirror. There had been rumors of a merger or acquisition flying around lately, while her employer, GreenTech, had been in talks with a venture capitalist firm and a larger technology company. It seemed like big changes were on the horizon, but she didn't know their extent. Considering she had been Vice President of Sales for almost three years, she felt relatively safe. But she couldn't help but question her judgment about that too.

At least she could have a glass of wine later with Brad to celebrate or commiserate. Or both, really.

How would she tell Brad?

In, out, in, out.

She dried her hands and checked her eye makeup. Time to put on a brave face.

Resolved, Adrian ran her fingers through long raven hair to freshen it up. Grabbing her black leather folder from the sink, she headed toward the meeting, strategically avoiding eye contact with everyone in the office. She distracted herself with a mental rundown of her team's sales figures and other talking points, getting ready for whatever questions were thrown her way.

When Adrian entered the board room, her eyes fell on a large canvas banner hung across the white board, proudly proclaiming, "It's a Boy!" with two tiny blue booties and a baby rattle framing the words. Blue and white confetti peppered the conference table, and her heart sank. They'd forgotten to clean the room after Michelle's baby shower.

She had felt pure excitement for Michelle earlier, having brought her one of those cakes made of diapers, with blue and yellow ribbons and ducks and all the cutesy adornments. Michelle and the other ladies in the office had cooed over it, almost in sync.

"I can't wait to bring one of these to your shower," Michelle beamed.

"Hopefully soon. Who knows?" Adrian said, patting her stomach gently. Other women gave her hopeful glances, knowing full well how long Adrian had been trying for a baby of her own. She'd even allowed herself to envision what kind of baby shower her colleagues would throw for her. She'd opt for cupcakes instead of the sheet cake Michelle asked for and would have them arranged in the shape of a stork carrying a bundle of joy. She even mused about doing a gender reveal through the cake. Each cupcake would contain either pink or blue frosting in the middle, a confectionery surprise with every bite, which they'd all take together on the count of three.

"Oh my gosh. You're having a boy *and* a girl!" Diane would exclaim.

"Twins! Congratulations. No one deserves it more," Michelle would gush.

What a fantasy.

Adrian pulled the banner down and threw it in the trash and then she swept the confetti off the table, eliminating the macabre evidence. She settled on the left side of the large oak conference table into a white space-age wingback chair reminiscent of one a sci-fi villain might use. She peered out at the Austin skyline, watching the afternoon sun shimmer against the neighboring highrises.

She grabbed her cell phone to text Brad, unable to carry the burden on her own any longer. Then she paused. Was texting really an appropriate way to tell him? He knew as well as she did how regular her monthly cycle was. They'd spoken about its punctuality ad nauseam for months. At first, she'd stayed positive, convinced her body was detoxing from the pill. But that excuse didn't work after six months. Every time they weren't fruitful, they deflated a little more, their hearts becoming flat and unmoving, with nothing left to give.

People started filing into the room. She typed out, "*Not this month*," and hit send before placing her phone face down. She turned her attention to Simon, her boss, ready to hear what else fate had in store.

He addressed the group. "Good afternoon." The afternoon sun reflected off his bald head as he wrote a word on the white board at the front of the room. Adrian's pulse quickened when she saw the word *Byte-Tech* scribbled in red marker.

So, the rumors were true?

"I'm sure some of you are aware that we've been in negotiations with Byte-Tech for a couple of months now, and we've finally been able to reach an agreement. We will be joining forces with them at the beginning of our new fiscal year in October."

A few of her cohorts shifted in their seats, and Adrian's phone buzzed. She flipped it over to see a response from Brad: "*Sorry, babe.*"

Simon carried on discussing the findings from the consultants they'd hired to ensure the merger would be a success, and it sparked something in Adrian. GreenTech had hired consultants to help with the merger with Byte-Tech. Wasn't it time for her and Brad to do something similar?

While Simon's back was turned, she quickly responded to Brad. "*Should we make an appointment with Holly?*"

Holly Dunham was the top fertility expert in the greater Austin area. If anyone could help them bear fruit, it would be her. Adrian had read many Holly-related success stories on various Austin mommy blogs during one of her sleepless nights. Adrian had mentioned the idea to Brad a few months earlier, and he'd convinced her to hold off a little longer to see if things happened naturally. Adrian couldn't help feeling put off at the time, but they'd keep trying, hoping for the best. But it was time for them to face facts. Neither of them were getting any younger, so a fertility appointment had to be the next logical step for them.

While Simon assured everyone their jobs were secure, Adrian watched her screen as Brad typed and stopped typing several times. Surely, he couldn't say no. But he wasn't saying anything at the moment—the three dots showed up and disappeared over and over again as he began to type and stopped. Was it a new form of Morse code?

"Adrian, will you share with us the projected sales numbers for your team for the remainder of the quarter?" Simon asked.

She cleared her throat as a simple *"Okay"* came across her phone screen.

She flipped the phone over a little too hard, startling her neighbor. "Yes, we're on track for our best year and quarter-end yet," she said. She reviewed the details with her colleagues on which sales campaigns had provided the most impact and reviewed high-level details on the top five deals set to close.

"Thank you." Simon grinned. "I want to commend you on your ability to keep your team focused on closing business while the rumor mill churned about the merger. We'll be leaning on you while we bring the two sales teams together." His expression practically confirmed she would be appointed Vice President of Sales over the combined sales teams moving forward, and the nodding heads in suits around the table agreed.

"Thank you, sir," she said, feeling heat flush her cheeks. In her thirty-something years alive, she'd never been comfortable taking a compliment.

As Simon moved on to question Patrick from Technical Support, Adrian exhaled a breath she hadn't realized she'd been holding. She'd successfully built her sales team to produce record-breaking numbers month after month, and it had taken her years to get to that point in her career. She'd been proud of her accomplishments and seeing her team's success and growth.

Now she just needed to figure out what was necessary to grow a baby.

SALTED water roared and meat sauce splattered the white quartz countertop like a Pollock painting as Adrian stared out her kitchen window. Where had they gone wrong that month? She'd held her legs in the air after every coitus experience with Brad for at least ten minutes. She'd kept tabs on her cycle with absolute precision, making sure they capitalized on the precise window of optimal fertility regardless of potential excuses. What was wrong with her?

Maybe it was time to consider alternatives. Maybe they needed a little boost. She remembered Samantha in her yoga class mentioning having success with IVF. Adrian had had a really good year at work, so affording the treatment shouldn't be an issue, regardless of whether or not her insurance would cover a portion.

But why had Brad started to text and stopped so many times? Those repeating three dots taunted her several times before the simple response of "Okay" came through. Was he holding something back? Was he truly onboard with going down the path of fertility treatments?

They'd always envisioned being parents. They'd discussed how many children they would have the night before their wedding. Being a risk-averse person, she remembered going to see him, saying they needed to hash out the main issues couples argue about before they walked down the aisle the next afternoon. The last thing she wanted to do was fail at marriage. They'd stayed up until three in the morning discussing how they would handle finances, when they would buy a house and what criteria were important to them, how many children they would have and to what lengths they would go to in order to produce them naturally. They'd agreed to consider fertility treatments if all else failed and would cap it after a year if nothing happened. But they were sure when the time came, it wouldn't be an issue.

Yet, there they were, and she felt less than confident about his response.

Maybe she was just imagining things. She knew Brad was under a lot of pressure at work, having recently started a new job in sales for a large wine distributor. She'd been removed from working a territory for a long time and could see the wear on him when he came home. It was an exhausting grind, and she should be more sensitive to that. But something told her there was more to it. She couldn't explain it, but she felt it. Call it women's intuition or whatever, but something felt off.

Brad entered the kitchen, immediately turning the heat down to keep the sauce from splattering. "Babe, are you okay?" He placed a warm hand on her shoulder, pulling her into a hug as tears streamed down her cheeks. He rubbed her back as she buried her head in his shoulder, using his shirt to soak up her pain.

"Do you still want to have children?" She looked into his honey brown eyes.

He brushed dark hair back from her face. "Of course."

He said the right words, but she didn't believe him. *Dot, dot, dot...*

"Are you sure?"

He nodded. "But is now really the right time? I just started a new job, and you've got the merger happening. Maybe we should wait."

There it was. She'd known she wasn't crazy. She pulled away from him. "Babe, we both know there's never going to be a 'right time.' And we're not getting any younger..."

"Yeah, you're right." He looked at the ground and leaned against the kitchen island.

Silence hung heavy between them as Adrian dropped the spaghetti into the boiling water, watching it swirl around her bamboo spoon as she stirred.

"Have we really done everything we can to make it happen naturally?"

She dropped the spoon on the counter. "I knew it. You've changed your mind, haven't you?"

"What do you mean?"

"We've already discussed this. Don't you remember? The night before our wedding? We agreed when it got to a certain point, we would explore other options before it was too late."

"I just thought we could give it a bit more time—wait a little while longer."

"For what? What are we waiting for?" She stared at him, unable to understand what was causing him to delay the inevitable.

"You're right." He rubbed his forehead. "I'm tired, you're tired, and I don't want to argue. If this is what you want—"

"I do."

"Okay, then we'll explore those options."

"Okay." She finished putting dinner together. His lips expressed the right words, but she couldn't help feeling he wasn't saying everything. But what would cause Brad to change his mind?

A tension-filled cloud hung over them with a light drizzle of conversation as they ate dinner side-by-side on barstools at the island. Brad offered to clean up the kitchen while Adrian headed to bed. She wanted to end the day as quickly as possible.

As Adrian tossed and turned that night, she realized Brad's behavior had been off lately. He'd had a lot of late nights at the office, coming home smelling like alcohol and a hint of perfume when he said he was entertaining clients. Could that have anything to do with his change of heart about their family plans?

He was holding something else back. She had to figure out what it was, even if it killed her.

2
_____

Brad shifted uncomfortably and pretended to read a two-month old copy of *Sports Illustrated*, flipping the pages at just the right speed to indicate he wasn't really reading. Adrian sat next to him, arms crossed and leg tapping, unable to focus on anything other than the fake ficus in the corner of the waiting room of Holly Dunham, fertility expert extraordinaire. Fortunately, Holly had a last-minute cancellation and they were able to grab an appointment that afternoon. Adrian hardly had time to think and quickly re-arranged meetings to make it happen. She hadn't even had a chance to talk to Laura about any of it yet.

Best friends since childhood, Laura and Adrian did everything together. When Laura got her ears pierced, Adrian did too. When Laura found Zach, it wasn't long until Adrian found Brad, even though Adrian beat Laura down the aisle. And when Laura had to follow Zach to Austin for his job, Adrian somehow convinced Brad to get on board with moving from Florida to Texas, the idea of being so far from Laura too much to bear. And when Laura announced her pregnancy, Adrian knew it wouldn't be long before they'd share the journey of motherhood too. Yet there she was in a fertility waiting room with vacancy in her own body's waiting room.

Smooth jazz elevator music played on repeat as they waited, unable to drown out Brad's page turning. He licked the tip of his finger before turning a page, and Adrian wondered where and when he'd developed such a habit. Aside from the unsanitary aspect, did it really provide more leverage on turning a thin page? Couldn't he just turn the page without the salivary theatrics?

She took a deep breath to calm her nerves. Pictures of happy couples stared at them out of frames on the walls, with both couples placing proud hands on the woman's swollen belly. Was that a preview of coming attractions? If Holly could work for those people, perhaps she would be able to wield her magic on them too.

"Adrian, Brad. Please come in," Holly said, opening the door.

Brad placed a slightly damp hand on the small of Adrian's back as they made their way to the woman's office.

Adrian felt a little calmer on the other side of the door. It was hard not to. Holly had decorated her office like a spa. The only color in the room was a pale green accent wall. Sheer, flowing white curtains hugged a window facing a lush, shady backyard. Her desk, a Quaker-style one made of rich mahogany, was in front of the window with a plush, cream-colored chair for Holly. Two matching chairs sat facing the window in front of her desk, and a large black and white photograph of stacked stones reminiscent of something from a big box store hung on the wall to the right. A diffuser puffed lavender scented steam into the room. The only thing missing was Enya or Yanni.

They took their seats, and Holly wasted no time diving in. "So, what brings you both here today?"

Adrian wondered why that was even a question. Wasn't

it obvious? "Well, we've been unsuccessful in our efforts to conceive, and we've agreed it's now time to explore our options."

Brad squirmed in his seat, drawing Adrian's attention to him. She couldn't help thinking about his shifty behavior lately, coming home smelling like alcohol when he was working late. Maybe she wasn't giving him enough credit. He was in sales for an alcohol distributor after all. A lot of deals got done on the golf course in the corporate world, so what would be the equivalent in his field? A bar?

"Babe?" Brad said.

"Sorry, what?"

"I asked if you've had any new stressors lately that could be interfering?" Holly's pen hovered above a yellow legal pad.

"No, not that I'm aware of." Adrian thought about the merger at work and the fact that she couldn't shake the idea Brad was hiding something. Oh, and her barren uterus. Other than that, things were peachy.

"And do either of you drink?"

"Yeah, we have a glass of wine a couple of nights a week," Brad said.

"Do you smoke?"

"No," Adrian answered too quickly. Brad raised an eyebrow. It was Adrian's turn to shift uncomfortably in her seat, afraid Brad would out her as a closet smoker.

"Regular periods?"

"Yeah, no issues there."

"And how was your mother's pregnancy with you?"

Adrian tensed. Her mother's pregnancy, from what details Adrian had pieced together over the years, hadn't been an easy one. "I—I don't recall." She hoped that would be the end of it.

"They haven't spoken in over three years," Brad volunteered.

Adrian restrained the urge to elbow him. Hard. What did that have to do with anything?

Holly's brow furrowed. "Well, you may want to consider talking to her. She could provide insight. Maybe she had a hard time conceiving you, and that information would be very helpful in creating a treatment plan."

The dread bubble in Adrian's stomach grew larger at the thought of having to talk to her mother. She wasn't ready to face that demon, let alone talk to her.

"When was your last physical?"

"About a year ago," Adrian replied, thankful to move on.

"We should start there. Let's run a full blood panel on you to see if there isn't an underlying issue that could be causing the difficulty conceiving. But I'd encourage you to talk to your mother and see if she has any information that could help."

"That sounds great." Brad stood. Adrian noticed beads of sweat pooling around his brow. What had gotten into him?

"I know this can feel like a lot, but we're in this together now, and I'm committed to helping you two have a baby." Holly reached her hand across the table and grabbed Adrian's. Her fingers were ice cold.

"Great, so we're done here?" Brad said.

"Clearly, *you* are," Adrian said. She made her blood panel appointment for later that week, and Holly reminded her to fast for twelve hours prior to it. Adrian thanked Holly for her time, and they left, Brad practically bolting for the door. Seething, Adrian prepared for a tense drive home.

———

Uncomfortable silence hung heavy between Brad and Adrian as he drove them home. Adrian started to speak several times but stopped, unsure of what to say. One thing was certain —Brad wasn't being honest. Maybe he'd changed his mind about having children and was afraid to let her down. The nagging feeling prodded her to speak. "Is everything okay?"

Brad sighed. "Honestly, no. I don't think this is going to work, and we should call it."

"But we haven't even tried yet. You heard Holly. We need to rule out other causes before—"

"I'm not talking about that. I'm talking about us." His voice cracked.

Adrian's jaw slacked. "What are you saying?"

He paused. "I think I want a divorce."

His words sucker punched Adrian. Her head spun and she saw stars. Divorce? Where was that coming from?

She looked out the window at the blurry lines on the road as memories flooded her vision. The fundraising event where they'd met—the one Laura had dragged Adrian to in spite of her protest of wanting to stay home. The silly date Laura bought for Adrian with Brad "for charity," despite Adrian not looking for a relationship and not interested in glorified prostitution, charities be damned.

Laura re-telling the story at her wedding as Adrian rolled her eyes and laughter filled the room.

The first time Brad said he loved her. His tender kisses on her forehead.

Making love on the beach in Punta Cana during one of her sales award trips.

The way he used to keep her awake with his snoring, but how she could no longer sleep without the noise.

How he wrapped her in his arms to keep her warm when the temperature dropped below 70.

The excitement when they moved into their house, quickly agreeing which room would be the nursery.

Their honeymoon in Cabo, where they spent the entire trip in their room exploring every curve of each other's bodies. She'd told Brad she wanted to go back at some point and actually experience Mexico, but life got in the way and they never made it.

Now they never would.

This couldn't be happening. This wasn't her life. This wasn't reality.

She could see Brad in her periphery, waiting for some kind of response. She thought about how his habits had changed in the last six months when he started his new job. He'd brushed it all off as pressure from work, and he worked later and later, some nights not getting home until well after nine. She'd never thought anything of it and always took him at face value. Was he lying that whole time? How could she be so stupid?

"Adrian?"

"Is there someone else?" She really didn't want to know. She knew better than to ask a question if she wasn't prepared to hear the answer. But she already knew. That had to be what he was hiding. The shark lurking beneath the surface, pulling her marriage down by its meaty calf dangling in the water.

"That...doesn't matter."

"Wow, seriously?" She crossed her arms over her chest, fighting back tears. Relief swept over her in the way it does when one hears the truth, regardless of its sting.

At least it was out in the open.

Knowing him, he probably loved the other woman. Who was she, anyway? She was probably some cliché, like a receptionist or bartender with long blond hair and big tits who loved sports and gave enthusiastic blow jobs. Adrian looked down at her small chest. No wonder.

The mystery woman probably didn't have original thoughts, always going along with whatever Brad said or wanted to do. He probably ate it all up, thinking they had so much in common and how easy she made it for him. Clearly, Brad was having a mid-life crisis a little early.

Could Adrian fix it? Was therapy an option for them? Could she honestly consider forgiving his indiscretion? Her mind couldn't keep up with the barrage, overburdened trying to process what had just happened. "Who is she?"

He swallowed hard. "That's irrelevant."

Time to face the music. He'd played the final note on their duet, and it was a sad one.

"Humor me, please?"

She thought about their wedding vows, how he'd promised to love, honor and cherish her as long as they lived. He'd been her rock that day. He'd whispered, "It's us against the world, baby," as they walked away from the altar as husband and wife. Not having her mother there, despite their strained relationship over the years, was really tough and Brad knew it. And now she felt stupid for believing him. "Brad?"

"It's no one you know, okay?" He scratched the small patch of skin that covered his voice box like he always did when he was frustrated. She could typically read him like a book, but this was a twist she didn't see coming. Did she really know him at all?

They sat in silence. She couldn't wait to get away from him. Knowing he was having an affair made her feel exposed. The thought of being practically middle-aged and divorced made her cringe. "Can we at least annul the marriage?"

"Why?"

"It's not for me. It's for my mother."

He scoffed. "You mean the one you haven't spoken to in over three years?"

The last time she saw her mother was at her father's funeral. She'd told Adrian she shouldn't marry Brad. That she didn't have a strong enough character to bounce back from a failed marriage. She'd rather die than face her mother with the news they were getting divorced. Death would almost be easier.

"That's not the point," she said, looking at the car next to them. A family in an SUV matched their speed in the next lane over, a blond girl with pigtails strapped into a car seat in the back. She locked eyes with Adrian and waved, beaming proudly as she clutched her stuffed panda.

"Adrian, did you hear me?" He touched her arm to bring her back to the present.

Adrian's eyes grew wide as she glanced back at the road, unable to speak. He looked forward just as they collided with a semitruck that had swerved into their lane. In an instant, everything went black.

3

____

And then everything wasn't dark anymore. A white void encompassed Adrian, leaving her unable to discern any surroundings. An overwhelming wave of love washed over her, eliminating any feelings of concern as it wrapped around her bodiless body. She realized the absence of her physicality in the void.

Did I die?

"Technically, yes, but it's not quite your time."

Adrian turned to see a little girl no older than six sitting on a bench. She scooted over, implying Adrian should join her.

Adrian walked with trepidation to meet her greeter. The little girl didn't move, patiently waiting. As Adrian approached, she noticed the uncanny resemblance between herself and her new companion. Her raven hair was braided in pigtails, but hazel eyes countered Adrian's dark brown ones. As the girl smiled, Adrian noticed her mouth was different—fuller than her own. She wore a pink and yellow floral dress with white lace over the bodice, the colors so vibrant in the void.

"Please, sit," she said, patting the bench.

"Who are you?" Adrian asked. "Are you God?"

"No." She giggled. "He's very far away from here."

"Are you me?"

"No, but I guess you could say I'm a part of you."

Adrian's brow furrowed. "What does that mean?"

"Sit."

Adrian complied, and they sat in silence. Her mind tried to make sense of the surroundings, including her almost-mirrored companion. Was she in Heaven? *If this is all there is to Heaven, it's boring as hell.*

"You're neither in Heaven nor Hell."

How'd you do that?

I can read your thoughts.

Adrian crossed her arms over her chest, feeling exposed.

"This is a gateway—a crossroads, if you will."

At the mention of crossroads, Adrian's environment came into focus. Their bench was on a platform between two trains going in opposite directions.

"Ah, interesting choice."

"I did this?"

"Yes, you are the creator of your Universe."

Adrian didn't believe her.

Try it.

Adrian pictured what she always imagined Heaven looked like: a waterfall with a misty rainbow, blue sky adorned with cotton ball clouds, and lying in a field of daffodils. The environment around them changed to match her thoughts. They were no longer on the bench in the train station but were lying in the field Adrian brought to life. She laughed in disbelief, feeling the daffodils tickle her arms as they swayed in the warm breeze.

"See?"

"This is amazing." Tears of joy leaked from her eyes. She could get used to this, could easily make such a beautiful place her new home. Then she remembered the girl saying it wasn't quite her time, and her stomach dropped. "I don't want to leave."

"The choice is yours, but you have more you could do on Earth."

Adrian considered the statement, thinking about the things she still wished to accomplish. Her dream had always been to paint. Her father was a gifted artist, and the apple hadn't fallen far from the tree. She was a natural with a brush in her hand but chose to climb the corporate ladder instead after her mother discouraged her artistic abilities. *Your father is the artist of the family*, her mother said as she pushed Adrian toward a sales career. If she stayed, she'd never get the chance to leave her artistic mark on the world.

"There's more to it than just painting," the girl said.

Adrian thought about Brad and where they'd left off prior to her waking up in this place. "Did he make it?"

She shook her head. Before Adrian could react, she felt a wave of compassion from her companion. It helped calm her emotions before they could manifest. Guilt bubbled to the surface in spite of that, as Adrian realized they'd never finish their conversation. Had she distracted him too much? That semitruck had, in fact, swerved into their lane from out of nowhere, right?

"Don't doubt divine will." The girl placed a tiny hand on top of Adrian's. "Things always happen perfectly and at the perfect time, even when the mind perceives it as less than perfect."

Her truth-filled words packed a punch. Adrian's mind had a hard time perceiving such profundity from a girl who appeared to be no older than six. "So, what else is there for me to do?"

"Your mother needs your help."

Adrian tensed, sitting straight up. Every fiber of her

being, whatever her being was in that place, protested against the idea of doing anything for her mother.

"That's all I can share with you at this point, but her fate, and yours, are relying on you."

"I don't think she wants my help." Her mother never asked anyone for help and probably wouldn't accept it from her, especially after everything that had happened. She felt the tickle of daffodils against her skin and grazed the petals of a nearby flower with her fingertips. "I haven't talked to her in over three years, and my life's been better for it."

Adrian always envied friends who had solid relationships with their mothers. Her best friend Laura had a great relationship with her mother, who showered Laura with love growing up, encouraging her to be true to herself and chase her dreams. Laura's dreams changed as frequently as her underwear at times, but her mother did nothing but encourage her imagination and wonder, supporting her even through making the wrong decisions. She'd offer motherly words of caution and wisdom but allowed her daughter the freedom to make her own choices and, often, her own mistakes, learning from them along the way. Laura and her mother were still very close. Adrian often wished she'd been Laura's sister.

Unlike Laura, Adrian's relationship with her mother had always been a struggle. Adrian often received words of criticism from her mother, making her doubt her choices. She got the impression she wasn't overly thrilled to be her mom, pining for missed opportunities in a career cut short. On the other hand, her mother also seemed jealous about how close Adrian was to her father. But he was more of a nurturer. Adrian always wondered if she had been switched at birth. She couldn't see any relation between herself and her mother, the tart vinegar to her oil. The only reason she didn't insist on a maternity test was how much she had in common with her father; and her parents were sincerely devoted to one another. That and the striking physical resemblance between them, which probably saved them from strangling each other a time or two.

The girl shrugged. "It's ultimately your choice, but would you truly be at peace with unresolved conflict with your mother?"

Damn if the six-year old wasn't right. Part of Adrian had always longed to reach some form of common ground with her mother. She'd seen how good mother-daughter relationships could be, and if she stayed, the "what if" would eat away at her. If her marriage taught her anything, it was that everything bubbles to the surface eventually. She'd placed her issues with her mother on the back burner long enough.

Adrian sighed. "Okay, how does she need my help?"

"I cannot reveal that to you at this time, but you will find out soon enough." The girl looked off into the distance, as if hearing a message from an invisible source. "It's time for you to go back now."

A wave of fear rushed over Adrian. She wasn't ready to leave the perfect place. She'd never felt more alive, more loved, in her entire life. "I don't know if I can." Her voice was suddenly so small she didn't recognize it as her own.

"God is always with you." She peered into Adrian's eyes with compassion. "Just remember him, and you can experience this feeling whenever you wish."

"Will I ever see you again?" She felt a sudden attachment to her almost-mini-me.

"Before you know it." She smiled, leaning over to kiss Adrian's forehead. Adrian closed her eyes and felt like she was falling backward, a heaviness sinking in with her descent. Then pain.

Excruciating pain.

She couldn't lift any of her limbs. Everything felt so

heavy. She struggled to open her eyes and could hear the hum of equipment around her. As her eyes blinked, she saw fluorescent lights. The sterile smell of antibacterial ointment and rubber gloves tickled her nose. She was in a hospital.

She heard a concern-laced voice from somewhere in the room.

No, it couldn't be. Could it?

Adrian groaned, and the voice stopped.

"She's awake!" the voice cried out to the hospital staff. "Come quick! She's awake! What are you doing just standing there? Didn't you hear me?"

It was definitely Adrian's mother.

Why did she choose to come back again?

4

Margaret Russo sat in a sterile hospital room holding her daughter's hand, willing her to wake up. The rhythmic beeping of machines assured her life still touched her daughter's broken body, but she watched the steady rising and falling of her chest to be sure. Besides, technology could be wrong and was known to fail every now and then.

She'd remained steadfast by Adrian's side for the last five days with no change. She'd ignored Laura's invite to get a good night's sleep at her house. She didn't want to miss a thing, although her diet of coffee and stale pastry wasn't going to cut it much longer. She knew she was in for a tongue-lashing from her doctor when she got home.

The doctors said Adrian would be fine. She'd been stable for three days but refused to wake up, as stubborn as she was. Margaret wasn't above shaking her to bring her back if need be. She might have to resort to that if it were much longer. She'd rescheduled her next doctor's appointment twice and couldn't push it off again. She wasn't thrilled at the idea of finding out what was wrong with her, but she needed to face that inevitable music. Until then, she'd enjoy her bliss-filled ignorance while she still could.

As she watched Adrian's chest rise and fall, it reminded her of watching her breathe while she slept in a crib as a baby. Margaret had often resisted the urge to poke her until she cried to make sure she was still alive. She'd been terrified to bring her baby home and never felt those maternal instincts she was supposed to have. She'd felt incomplete as a woman, unable to relate to her friends who happily took care of babies and the household, always had dinner on the table by six pm, and never gave a second thought to a career.

She should consider herself lucky. A career wasn't even an option for *her* mother, so the fact that Margaret had that choice was a blessing. But she'd gone and fallen in love with an artist, and someone needed to provide for them. And boy, did she fall. They were inseparable, thick as thieves, always supporting each other's dreams and endeavors. They found it practically impossible to say no to one another, always finding a way to make things work through hair-brained schemes and eventual flops.

She never gave George enough credit. He did everything imaginable to take care of her and Adrian, even to his detriment. He was always more of the nurturer out of the two of them, and nothing was more important to him than his family. He never brought his stress home, even when he would juggle two or three jobs at a time. He carried the load of everything like a pack mule when Margaret had a hard time functioning, let alone working, after Adrian was born. He was the epitome of a gentleman, and she missed him every day. Three years hadn't made it any easier to be alone.

Adrian was so angry at Margaret when George died, blaming her for hiding how sick her father was. But in Margaret's defense, she didn't know either. He hid the severity of his condition well until it was too late, brushing her off and insisting he was fine. Things happened so quickly that it left her shell-shocked. But maybe Adrian was right. How could Margaret not have known? She'd replayed their last week together over in her mind until the memories wore out, not able to pinpoint what led to her husband's departure. But how could she have predicted his heart giving out? Perhaps he'd given all he could and there was nothing left to make his ticker tick. It was one of God's many mysteries.

She and Adrian hadn't spoken since the funeral. Both of them were already angry at God for taking away the most important man in their lives, and then Margaret had gone and made things worse by sharing her true thoughts about Brad. In hindsight, even after not speaking to Adrian for over three years, Margaret stood by what she'd said. Although she could have chosen her words more carefully and perhaps even addressed her concern at a different time and place. But she was right about Brad. God rest his soul.

What words would she use to tell her daughter her husband didn't survive their accident?

"Any change?" Laura interrupted Margaret's thoughts as she entered the room.

Margaret shook her head. "Not yet."

Laura took a seat in the corner and they listened to the noise from the monitors and machines. They'd grown comfortable together in silence over the last couple of days, waiting patiently for signs of life from Adrian. Margaret was so thankful Laura reached out and told her what happened. She and Laura had a semi-regular cadence of keeping in touch over the last three years. She'd call Margaret and fill her in on details of Adrian's life—her and Brad's fertility issues, her promotions at work, and all the mundane stuff in between. She even told Margaret about Adrian trying out bangs in a new haircut, quickly realizing it wasn't a good look for her. She'd laughed as Laura told her all the creative ways Adrian wore hats to cover it up until her hair grew out.

When Laura called a few days earlier, Margaret had assumed it was their normal cadence until she heard a tearful, shaky explanation of what happened. Margaret didn't hesitate to fly out on the next flight to Austin, immediately regretting not reaching out to Adrian over the last three years. Would she ever have the chance to talk to her daughter again?

"What time is your flight back?" Laura asked.

"At five-thirty." Margaret looked at the clock. She needed to head toward the airport to ensure she didn't miss the flight. But Adrian still wasn't awake. She couldn't leave yet. She needed to see her daughter wake up and know for certain she would be okay. She couldn't leave her tied to the spaghetti mess of cords and machines with a clear conscience.

"You know you can't miss this appointment again."

"I know." Margaret gripped Adrian's hand a little tighter.

"She's receiving excellent care here. You have to take care of you too."

Margaret nodded. "You're right." She reluctantly released her daughter's hand. Blood rushed to her head when she stood, and the room came back into focus through the momentary void. "This is just like her. So stubborn." She laughed nervously.

"I promise I'll let her know you were here when she wakes up. She's going to wake up." Laura placed a hand on Margaret's shoulder.

As if on cue, something stirred in the corner of her eye. Margaret saw life wiggle back into Adrian's motionless body. Her daughter groaned. She was awake. Alive. She felt pain, and it was wonderful.

"She's awake!" Margaret cried out to the hospital staff. "Come quick! She's awake!"

5

———

"Ma?"

"Yes, I'm here." Margaret squeezed Adrian's hand, which lay limp, lacking the strength to squeeze back.

"But...what happened?"

"From what we gathered, you slammed into a semitruck. Doctors said your pelvis cracked, and they had to remove your spleen. You also cracked three ribs on your right side. It's amazing that you're still alive." Margaret's eyes looked glassy as she brushed hair back from Adrian's forehead.

No wonder she felt so much pain.

As Margaret spoke, Adrian's eyes came into focus. Something was off. She resisted the urge to pinch Margaret, finding it hard to believe she was real. Her mother had lost a significant amount of weight. She now had a salt and pepper pixie cut instead of long locks twisted up in a bun. More wrinkles carved into the smoothness of her now pallid complexion. The changes seemed more drastic than three years of aging should. *Your mother needs your help.* The child's words echoed in her mind.

"Why'd you come?"

"Really, Adrian? You almost died. Shouldn't that be enough of a reason for us to end our...disagreement?"

Adrian studied her mother more closely. Bags hung heavy under her eyes, like she'd been in a bar fight. Given the circumstances, she probably hadn't been sleeping, but what was going on beneath the surface? She clearly wasn't well. Had she come to apologize on Adrian's death bed? Was it too late to go back to sleep?

"Adrian?"

"You don't look well."

"Look who's talking." Margaret coughed. It took her a minute to find her breath.

"Are you okay?"

"I'm fine." She waved a hand. "Enough about me. I hate to be the one to tell you this, but—"

"Brad didn't make it, did he?"

She shook her head, affirming what Adrian already knew. Margaret apologized as tears leaked down the sides of Adrian's face. Margaret placed a wrinkled hand on top of Adrian's to provide some comfort, and they sat in silence for a few moments.

"Knock, knock." A tall, slender man in green scrubs peered into the room. "Mrs. Foley, glad to see you're awake." He approached her bedside, gray hair poking out from his scrub cap. "I'm Dr. Barnes." He gently touched her hand, his skin soft and nails perfectly manicured. "You survived quite an accident, my dear." He had a slight Canadian accent.

"Yeah, my mom just told me what happened."

He nodded, his deep blue eyes full of kindness. "Do you want the good news or bad news first?"

"Tell me somethin' good," she said, wincing from pain as she tried to sit up.

"Easy there." He laid her back. "So, the good news is your pelvis suffered only a hairline fracture, which will cut your recovery time to about six to eight weeks. You should be able to walk out of here in about a week, though. With some help, of course."

"A week?"

"Yeah, that's the bad news." He grimaced. "You had a lot of internal bleeding from the accident, and I had to perform an open splenectomy, so I'm going to need to keep an eye on you for another week."

Adrian paused. "Will I be okay without a spleen?"

"Oh, yeah, you'll be fine. But your immune system could be compromised, so you will be more prone to infection moving forward."

"And how long until I can go back to work?" The launch. The merger. Adrian's pulse raced.

"I'm going to need you to take it easy for at least four weeks. Preferably six."

"How easy?"

"Have you heard of Netflix?" He smiled.

She giggled. "Don't make me laugh." Her face contorted into something between a smile and a wince as pain radiated through her body.

"Sorry." Definitely Canadian. "Do you have any other questions for me right now, my dear?" Adrian shook her head. "Okay, I'll come by tomorrow to check on your progress. Hang in there, kiddo." He put her chart back on the door and left.

She took a moment to process everything Dr. Barnes had said, a sinking feeling washing over her. She knew how critical a time it was for the company, and not being a part of it, even for reasons like barely surviving a life-threatening accident, would be severely frowned upon.

"Hey, sleepyhead." Laura approached her bedside. "How are you?"

"Spectacular." A smile tugged at her lips.

"Glad to see your sarcasm is intact."

"That's about all that is right now, apparently."

"First step on the road to recovery." She smiled, touching Adrian's arm. Despite the circumstances, Laura looked absolutely beautiful and put together, her dark curly hair without any frizz.

"I'll leave you be," Margaret said, touching Adrian's hand once more before struggling to stand. Laura helped her find her balance. "There's a flight back in a couple of hours, and I need to be on it."

Adrian felt a jolt radiate through her body at Margaret's touch, seeing a vision of her mother dying. Alone. The flash only lasted a moment. What was that?

"You're leaving?" Adrian knew much more needed to be said, but the words refused to flow.

"Yeah, I have some commitments back in Florida I need to attend to, and you're in good hands here, so..."

In Adrian's condition, she had no choice but to let her mother go. She didn't have the strength to make her stay.

"I'll call you when I get home," Adrian said. Margaret nodded, leaning over to kiss her daughter's forehead with dry lips. When she got to the doorway, Margaret turned back and forced a smile that did nothing to mask the pain in her eyes. Then she left.

"I'm surprised she came." Adrian had known she'd see her mother again at some point, but the reunion was the farthest thing from her imagination. And now that it had happened, an empty feeling sank in as she realized how much she'd missed having her mother around. Or at the very least, the idea of her. Maybe the second chance was not only for her but also for her mother. Adrian had changed a lot in the last few years. Maybe Margaret had too.

"You're her daughter. Despite the past, nothing changes that."

"She couldn't wait to leave, though."

"She came. Doesn't that count for something?" Laura was right. Margaret was never good with apologies, so maybe being there was her olive branch.

"Did she look well to you?" Adrian asked.

"She has COPD."

"COPD?"

"Basically, her lungs are inflamed, making it difficult for her to breathe. All those years of smoking have taken their toll on her." Laura gave her a sideways glance, knowing Adrian was a closet smoker. She only smoked when stressed. Or nervous. Or happy. So, it really didn't count.

"How do you know all of this?"

"We had some time to catch up while you were sleeping." Laura tucked a strand of hair behind Adrian's ear.

Somehow, Adrian didn't feel like she was getting the whole story, but maybe the pain meds were making her paranoid.

"Don't worry too much. She has a really good doctor back home." Laura placed a hand on Adrian's forearm.

"I hope you're right." Concern spread across Adrian's face as guilt settled in for neglecting her mother. She debated telling Laura about her experience on the other side but decided to wait.

"Well, you're in no condition to do anything about it right now, so just get some rest, and take care of you. Can I bring you anything? Ice chips or something?"

Adrian nodded. "Ice chips."

"You got it." Laura squeezed her arm. "I'm glad you're back."

"Me too."

Laura's face turned serious. "Don't ever scare me like that again, okay?"

"I promise." She knew in her bones, the ones still intact anyway, that it was true.

————

BEING able to leave the hospital felt liberating. Adrian had been granted parole, and she was ready to experience freedom from the cell she'd been locked up in for over a week. Although she'd be leaving jail and heading home to be imprisoned by memories of what was and thoughts of what could have been. That, and the doctor told her she'd be on a heavy physical therapy regimen for several weeks and should add plenty of shows to her Netflix queue.

"Are you sure you don't want to come stay with us for a while?" Laura asked.

"No, I'll be fine. Besides, you have a baby to take care of, and I don't want to burden you."

"You're never a burden, and you know it."

They drove away from the hospital in silence. Adrian suspected Laura was waiting for her to change her mind, but she wouldn't. She needed to get used to being alone. Laura pulled into the parking lot of a big box store to pick up Adrian's meds while she waited in the car.

"Hey, will you get me a cane too?" Adrian held out her credit card. Laura nodded but refused to take the card, sticking out her tongue as she shut the door.

Adrian tugged at her seatbelt, realizing it was the main reason she was still alive. Without it, her fate could have been similar to Brad's. She knew the road to recovery would be steep, and she'd have trouble getting around for a while, but she could do it. Laura said she'd help as much as she could, but Adrian didn't expect her to drop everything at a moment's notice.

She rolled her window down, feeling the abnormally

warm October breeze tickle her skin. Sitting for any length of time wasn't the most comfortable, and she closed her eyes, ignoring the pain screaming out to be medicated.

The popping of the trunk startled her, and she looked in the rear-view mirror. She assumed Laura was hidden behind the towering bags of groceries she carefully slid into the trunk, balancing a cane on top of it all. Adrian smiled, wondering how she'd ever gotten so lucky to have such a great friend.

Laura quickly navigated the back roads to avoid traffic. "Almost there." She turned into the neighborhood, and Adrian could smell her neighbor's freshly cut grass as he mowed meticulous lines in his yard. She recognized the rows of houses with their brick and stone facades, and familiarity set in. Everything about it looked exactly as she remembered, and she exhaled.

"Home sweet home." Laura pulled into the driveway. Adrian looked at her limestone two-story house and her heart sank. The windows peered right through her, sending a shiver down her spine. She knew it was her home, but it looked so cold and foreign to her.

Laura walked around to help her out, and she considered changing her mind about staying with Laura instead. Could she really face the big house alone?

"You okay?"

Adrian nodded, words escaping her. She handed her keys to Laura, who jiggled the lock to open the door. Adrian crossed the threshold, pictures of her and Brad greeting her from a nearby wall. She felt nauseous.

"Whew, let's turn on some AC," Laura said as a wave of stuffy, stale air hit them. She adjusted the thermostat and helped Adrian get settled on the plush sofa in her living room. Laura went to grab the groceries, leaving Adrian alone in the cavernous space. Vaulted ceilings in the living room now seemed like a bad decision. She felt so small in the enormity of the house.

"Where do you want me to set you up?" Laura set the bags of groceries down on the kitchen island.

All four of the bedrooms were on the second floor, and Adrian considered the stairs for a moment. She remembered when she and Brad first looked at the house. Laura had sold it to them, and Adrian initially thought it was too big. Brad assured her it had plenty of room to grow into as they started their family, and they'd quickly agreed which room would be the nursery. She wasn't prepared to go upstairs, and the thought of climbing into bed with sheets that still smelled like him made her stomach turn.

"Adrian?"

"I think I'll stay down here." Adrian turned away from the ghosts haunting the second floor, feeling relieved to have a sleeper sofa as Laura pulled out the couch. Laura created a nest, loaded with cozy blankets and lots of pillows she'd retrieved from a linen closet upstairs. Adrian slowly crawled into her new bed, and Laura set her up with anything she could possibly need nearby, including snacks, the TV remote, and her cell phone.

"Are you sure about this?"

Adrian nodded. "I just need to rest."

"Okay. I'll come by later to check on you." She tucked Adrian into the blankets. "Love you."

"Love you more." Adrian blew Laura a kiss, and she left. The door shut and the lock clicked home.

Adrian looked over at her provisions, seeing a picture of her with Brad from their wedding day in a silver frame. They were both smiling, gazing longingly into each other's eyes. She reached over to face it down and knocked it over instead, the glass shattering like her marriage.

She was officially alone.

She burst into tears, the finality of recent events sinking in. They'd never get to finish that conversation in the car, and she'd never get the answers to her barrage of questions. She'd never have closure. Never know why he'd betrayed her.

It hurt to cry because her ribs were still healing, but she couldn't stop. Once she opened the floodgates, so many emotions poured out. She still loved Brad and couldn't believe he was gone. Where did she go wrong? Was she really that bad of a wife?

It was her fault. She'd pushed him away in pursuit of her career. She should have spent more time with him. Should have been more supportive. Maybe if she'd been more vocal, more honest, things would have been better between them. Maybe if she had done that, he wouldn't have cheated. Maybe he wouldn't be dead.

But then again, he was the one who'd decided to cheat. He chose to seek comfort in the arms of someone else instead of working on things at home. Those were his choices to make, not hers.

What about their vows? Did they mean nothing? They felt like empty promises.

Pain coursed through her veins, and she took shallow breaths in a feeble attempt to calm her nerves. She needed to find a way to self-soothe and knew with time she'd get past all her wounds. She closed her eyes, wishing it were all a dream. The hum of the refrigerator lulled her to sleep.

6

A couple of weeks after being released from the hospital, Adrian felt restless from house arrest. She wondered how much longer she'd be sentenced to imprisonment, sharing a cell with Brad's shadow: his laundry, a bottle of his favorite craft beer in the fridge, smiling photos from their wedding day, and a few stray clippings from his electric razor around the bathroom sink. Death would have almost been easier, but every day, the pain subsided little by little, both physically and emotionally. She felt ready for parole, longing to establish a new form of normal without the ghosts.

She'd felt mixed emotions at his funeral a few days earlier. Paul and Rhonda waited until Adrian was physically able to attend a memorial for their son, and Laura acted as her physical and emotional crutch. The service was closed casket, and Adrian gave silent thanks for that small blessing. She didn't think she could hold it together seeing his lifeless body peacefully sleeping.

The memorial service felt like a weird dream. A blur of people came up to her, sharing their condolences, and she felt bile rise in her throat at the mention of Brad being a devoted husband. Despite it all, she couldn't bring herself to defile his memory and kept his infidelity swept under the rug. She'd scanned the room, searching for the other woman, but if his mistress was there, she hid her identity well. At least their vows stayed intact: *'Til death do us part.*

Laura texted, saying she was on her way over with dinner. She'd been a complete angel, shuttling Adrian to doctors' appointments in between taking care of her husband and son. She offered to help Adrian sort through Brad's things as well, when she felt up to it. Adrian considered taking her up on that, at least for an hour here and there. Besides, she'd grown tired of vegging in front of the television and needed to channel her energy into something productive.

Her mind felt idle since she hadn't received clearance to return to work yet. She longed for the distraction of helping her staff with deal cycles, achieving victory one sale at a time. However, the idea of going back to a corporate job felt empty somehow. Since her brush with death, she'd put her life under a microscope, moving everything into sharper focus. Knowing firsthand how fragile life was, what did she want to do with whatever time she had left? She hadn't quite figured it out, but she knew whatever it was probably had nothing to do with sales.

Regardless, she still had to make the donuts, so she called her boss to check in. "My doctor said I could probably return part-time in about three weeks or so." She shifted on the couch. Finding a comfortable position post-accident was still a challenge. When Simon didn't respond, she continued, "He recommended I start back part-time and see how I handle that for a couple of weeks before clearing me to return full-time." Dead air from the other end. "Simon?"

He sighed. "Look, there isn't an easy way to put this." Adrian's stomach dropped, anticipating the blow. "With the launch of version 3.0, we really need all hands on-deck, and the board is growing concerned about your ability to perform and lead a team during a very critical time in our business."

Her pulse raced. "What are you saying?"

"If you can't return full-time starting next week, we have no choice but to seek a replacement."

A replacement? He couldn't be serious. Who would be more dedicated than her? She'd poured her heart and soul into building her team, sacrificing her relationship at times for what she called *the bigger picture*. And what good had it done?

When she didn't answer, he continued, "We're prepared to offer you six months of severance pay if you're not able to return."

"Six months? That's it?" What a slap in the face.

"I'm sorry, Adrian. My hands are tied."

She sighed. After everything she'd done for the company, it was all for naught. And six months was an insult. But she'd played the game from the other side too many times not to know it wasn't negotiable. "I guess I have no other choice, do I?"

"I'm sorry."

"Me too."

When they hung up, Adrian stared at her phone's blank screen. Six months of pay wouldn't get her very far, especially with the mounting medical bills for both her and Brad. She wasn't in any condition to job hunt at the moment either.

But maybe she wouldn't have to.

She remembered Brad had a small life insurance policy from his job, which would probably cover their medical expenses with a little bit left over. Was the Universe actually conspiring in her favor, pushing her toward what she'd always wanted to do? If there was ever a time to do it...

"Hey, beautiful, dinner is here." Laura walked through the front door. She balanced a bag of food under one arm and her nine-month old son Dylan in the other. She placed the bag on the kitchen island and saw Adrian sitting motionless on the couch. "What's wrong?"

"I just talked to my boss. If I'm not able to return full-time next week, they're going to hire a replacement."

"What? No way. I'm so sorry, sweetheart." Laura sat next to her. "Are they at least offering you severance?"

"Six months."

Dylan whined.

"My sentiments exactly, kid."

Laura found his pacifier and put it in his mouth. "That's all?"

Adrian nodded. "I'm not sure what I'm going to do."

Laura paused. "What about selling the house? I'm sure you have a decent amount of equity, right?"

"I'd been thinking about that, actually." Selling the house would certainly take some pressure off. She and Brad had opted for mortgage insurance in the event of a death, so she'd own the house free and clear soon enough. And she was tired of living with ghosts. "Good thing I know a good realtor." She winked.

"Aww, shucks." Laura smiled. She offered to look into comparable sales and run some numbers later that evening. "Hey," she said, grabbing Adrian's hand. "You're going to get through this. *We* will get through this."

"I know. It's just a lot of change at once."

"If anyone can handle it, you can. You always find a way to come out of a shitty situation smelling like roses."

"Not in front of the baby." Adrian gasped, placing her hands over his tiny ears. They both laughed.

"Have you called your mom yet?"

Adrian cringed. "No. I should probably rip that Band-Aid off too."

"I think this little dude might need a diaper change," Laura said, getting up from the couch. She walked with Dylan toward the staircase. "See? Now you can call your mom."

"Great." Adrian stared at her phone. She remembered telling her mother she would call, but for some reason, had hesitated every time she went to dial the number. Margaret obviously knew Adrian didn't die from the accident. Did she really need any further update?

But you told her you would call her. The nagging voice squeaked from the back of her mind. Being a woman of her word, Adrian took a deep breath as she prepared to—

Her phone rang. The caller ID said Mom.

"Good to know you're still alive."

"Sorry I didn't call sooner."

"You didn't call at all. I called you."

"Okay…" Adrian trailed off. "H-how are you?"

Margaret sighed. "Not good."

"Look, I'm really sorry I didn't call."

"It's not that."

Adrian's pulse raced.

"Look, this is not the call I wanted to make, but I thought you had a right to know that my doctor says I have cancer."

Adrian's body stiffened. Her mother dropped the cancer bomb like it was something totally ordinary, like a rainstorm blowing in off the Gulf or forgetting to buy laundry detergent at the store. The casualness of it all caught Adrian completely off-guard. "What? How?"

"He found two tumors in my lungs during a routine checkup appointment. He took a biopsy to be sure. I got the results and sure enough, it's cancer."

A pit formed in Adrian's stomach. Cancer, really? She didn't know what to say. She could hear a television humming in the background. Apparently, the forecast in Florida called for partly cloudy skies and temperatures in the low 80s all week. She swallowed a lump in her throat. "What does that mean?"

"It's really not a big deal," Margaret said, recounting what her doctor shared. Adrian only heard the words *stage four, unknown prognosis,* and *positive outlook* from what her mother said. When she finished, they were silent, a commercial for denture cleaner in the background. "Okay, I better go."

Adrian didn't know what else to say, the weight of it all still floating on the surface. "Thanks for letting me know."

"I felt I owed it to you. I'll talk to you later."

"Mom?" She wasn't ready to hang up.

"What?"

"It's good to talk to you." Adrian twisted the hem of her over-sized music festival T-shirt.

She heard Margaret breathing on the other end of the line and sensed she wasn't the only one not wanting to break the connection. "Yep, you too. Okay, bye-bye."

Adrian stared at the black screen on her phone after she hung up. Had her mother gotten choked up, or was that her imagination? The cancer bomb left her feeling shell-shocked. She clenched her stomach as a wave of nausea washed over.

"What is it?" Laura asked.

"My mom has cancer," she blurted. Even saying the words out loud didn't make them seem more real. Was it all a dream?

Laura's face contorted into expressions of surprise and sympathy. She sat next to Adrian, gently grabbing her hand. "What did she say?"

"She had biopsies on two tumors in her lungs, and the doctor said they're cancerous." Adrian stared straight ahead while recounting what her mother told her, unable to make eye contact for fear of breaking down.

"I'm so sorry, hon." They were at a loss for words, cancer hanging heavy in the air. "What is she going to do?"

Adrian sighed. "I don't know. I forgot to ask."

"Who does she have in Florida?"

"I don't think she has anyone." Adrian's father passed away three years earlier, and she didn't have any siblings. Her mother had a few close friends, but she needed more than friends for a cancer diagnosis. She needed family, and the only family she had left was her daughter. An abyss grew in Adrian's stomach, the echo of the little girl's warning on the other side, *Your mother needs your help*, ringing in her mind.

Since Adrian was practically jobless, she knew what to do. The Universe was all but shoving her in that direction. "I guess it's all on me." She shrugged. "Is it just me, or does my life now resemble a sad country song?"

Laura chuckled. "If anyone can handle your mother, it's you."

"You sure about that?" Adrian raised an eyebrow. They both smiled.

Adrian's mind protested, memories flooding to the surface in an attempt to drown out the thought of going. Her mother certainly wasn't the easiest person to live with. She peppered Adrian with criticism, and nothing she ever did was quite up to Margaret's impossibly high standards. She heard her mother criticizing her care already. *Use the sponge with more force when you give me a bath, would you? No, rub the ointment clockwise, not counterclockwise. Forget it, I'll just do it myself.* Adrian shuddered. "I don't know if I can do this. My life hasn't been all that bad without her in it."

Laura looked at her sideways, calling her bluff. "Whatever, Adrian. Honestly, could you be at peace knowing your mother was dying all alone a thousand miles away?"

"When you put it that way, I'd be callous for saying yes." Adrian pouted like a petulant five-year old.

"I know you better than that. Regardless of the past, you would feel terrible knowing you didn't make some kind of peace with her before she dies."

Laura had a point. Adrian couldn't live with herself knowing she did nothing to help her mother. "You're right. I need to do this for me, as weird and selfish as that may sound."

"It doesn't sound *too* selfish," Laura teased. "But I know what you mean. You're making the right choice"

"I guess I should call her back and tell her I'm coming to stay with her." The words sounded so surreal leaving her lips.

"Do you want some privacy?"

"No, stay. This probably won't be long." She re-dialed her mother. "I think I should come stay with you for a while," she said when Margaret answered.

"Why?"

Like she didn't know? "To be honest, I'm about to get laid off from my job, so I thought it might be nice to come visit for a little while."

Margaret hesitated. "Okay."

Adrian knew by her mother's lack of interest in lecturing her about losing the job that Margaret's situation might be more acute than she'd led on. Adrian told her she'd have to get clearance from the doctor and tie up some loose ends over the next few weeks but would let her know when she was heading that way. Margaret agreed, and they hung up.

"What did she say?"

"She said okay. I guess I'm moving back in with my mother." Adrian grimaced.

"Maybe it won't be that bad."

Adrian shrugged. Laura obviously didn't remember much about Margaret.

———

MARGARET PULLED a pan of brownies out of the oven and placed them on a cork trivet to cool. She knew instinctively her friends would arrive any minute for their version of afternoon tea. She scanned her humble home for anything out of place, deciding they needed some background music to keep them company.

She turned the television from Fox News to a music channel playing old favorites and flashbacks from her youth. *Oh, what the hell*? She lit a sandalwood-scented candle. Satisfied, she returned to the kitchen to put on the kettle.

The doorbell rang, and Margaret greeted her friends Gilda and Bev. Gilda, a statuesque beauty with short red hair, and Bev, a stout brunette wearing a blue-knitted cap, had quickly become Margaret's version of family not long after she'd moved to Shady Acres a few years back. They'd met each other at one of the community's social events and were thick as thieves since. They'd supported one another through the loss of husbands, cancer diagnoses, arthritis and even boyfriends who'd come and gone. Gilda and Bev, survivors of melanoma and breast cancer respectively, vowed to support Margaret through her battle. It was her turn to survive cancer, just like the two of them had.

"You're looking well," Gilda said. "Have you started treatment?"

"Do I smell brownies?" Bev's eyes lit up.

"It wouldn't be tea without something sweet," Margaret said, avoiding Gilda's question.

They made their way to their usual seats at Margaret's round kitchen table, Margaret in the middle, Gilda on her left, and Bev to her right. They made small talk, allowing their tea to steep.

"So, when does Adrian arrive?" Bev asked.

"Tomorrow," Margaret replied. She folded and unfolded the corner of her napkin. A cacophony of emotions played in Margaret's anticipation of Adrian's arrival. While she didn't like the circumstances in which she and her daughter were reuniting, there was excitement at the opportunity to forge a better connection while she could. With age usually comes wisdom, and she'd had a lot of time to sit around and think about how she could have handled things differently.

"How many times have you checked things in her room?" Gilda asked.

"Oh, only about seven." She'd rearranged photos on the dresser three times, made and remade Adrian's bed twice with different sheets, and double-checked there were enough hangers in the closet.

"It's going to go well." Bev squeezed Margaret's hand.

"I hope you're right."

"How could she be wrong?" Gilda said.

"I've made mistakes in the past, and I—"

"Who hasn't?" Gilda cut her off. "No one is perfect, Margie."

Margaret sipped her tea, drinking in Gilda's words. She'd had plenty of time to think about the mistakes she made in the past, but she knew it wasn't healthy to dwell there either.

"Except Harold." Bev winked.

Margaret blushed. "I don't know what you're talking about."

"Oh please," Gilda said. "You two are like giddy teenagers when you see each other. Just ask him out already."

Margaret sat up straighter in her chair. "A lady doesn't ask."

Gilda's eyebrow raised. "Since when are you a lady?"

Margaret playfully slapped Gilda's hand. "You're one to talk." They all laughed. "Okay, who wants a brownie?"

7

Asun-faded sign welcomed Adrian back to the Sunshine State. Kudzu suffocated the trees flanking the highway, and her throat constricted. She'd forgotten how humid Florida was. The concept of drinking air summed it up. When she'd moved to Austin three years earlier, she'd vowed to never make the drive again. *Never say never*.

What transpired in the last three months had been referred to as a miracle on more than one occasion. Being an overachiever, she'd recovered faster than anyone expected, earning many figurative gold stars in physical therapy. Dr. Barnes said her immune system would be compromised the rest of her life, and she should expect some complications if she were to ever get pregnant. Not that that was high on her list of priorities anymore.

A lot of people were shocked to hear that she was doing such a long drive alone after nearly dying in a crash, but Adrian was a survivor, not a victim. She was determined to make the best of her circumstances, although she wasn't leaving much behind.

Laura helped her get rid of Brad's belongings and

prepare her house for the market. The listing would go live the next day, both of them agreeing it would be easier to sell it vacant. A flood of memories washed over her as she said goodbye to her old life and pulled out of the driveway for the last time. Laura insisted on seeing her off, saying, "parting is such sweet sorrow" as they hugged each other for the last time. They'd barely been apart since they were kids, and a reunion date was TBD. "You'll always have a home in Austin," Laura assured her. Adrian promised to call once she arrived.

Adrian couldn't bring herself to tell anyone except Laura about Brad's infidelity, and even that was a struggle. She didn't feel like she could tell anyone else. Like it would defile his memory. She'd wondered why she still felt such loyalty to a man who hadn't given her the same courtesy, but she couldn't help it. Despite everything, she still felt love for the man who left her with unanswered questions: How many times? Did he love the other woman? Did he no longer love Adrian? Where had she gone wrong?

At least he'd saved her the embarrassment of explaining his infidelity to everyone and declaring their marriage a failure. Obviously, she would have preferred he didn't die, and would have wished him well with whomever he chose to be with. But the way things played out had a finality that somehow made it a little bit easier to cope. She was finding her way forward, one day at a time.

Despite being disappointed at first, she'd come to realize what a blessing it was to lose her job. As much as she'd loved it, she felt like the proverbial square peg being shoved into the round hole of what she used to deem important. She no longer fit in her former life. The severance pay gave her an opportunity to find a new way, emerging as a magnificent butterfly from the husk of her former self. The unknowns excited and scared her simultaneously.

She followed a weather-beaten sign for the exit toward Sunview, her hometown. She shifted uncomfortably, the pain of sitting so long getting to her. She considered pulling over to stretch her legs but shook away the thought. She was too close to the end. She could push through.

She admired the sun's reflection, like diamonds off the water, as she drove over the intracoastal bridge. Fishermen cast their lines into the water at the north pier, earnestly hoping to catch something they could brag about over beers later. She rolled down her window, allowing the salty air to dance through her hair. She'd missed the ocean and its healing abilities and felt ready to be baptized anew in the salty water. She found it ironic that not too long ago, she couldn't wait to leave, and now she was literally soaking it all in. It wasn't just her aching body longing to be healed. The little girl's words beckoned her like a siren's call, reminding of her purpose: *Your mother needs your help*.

It was hard to fathom her mother needing anyone. The epitome of independent, Margaret held her cards close to the vest, hiding her emotions behind a thick outer shell. She'd told a young Adrian many times that she needed to toughen up—she was too soft, and the world would crush her if she stayed that way. Adrian needed to be like her if she wanted to survive. Adrian's father, George, praised her sensitivity, telling her it was okay to be as sensitive as she wanted to be. Adrian wondered on more than one occasion if her mother would have preferred having a boy or no child at all. Margaret wasn't the most nurturing, although Adrian wouldn't go as far to call her *Mommie Dearest* (she let her have wire hangers, after all). Adrian never felt comfortable talking to her mother about anything and usually went to her dad for advice and comfort. He never let Adrian down.

She turned down the familiar drag, passing The Pelican, its sign pink and cream, weathered with age. She and Laura had spent many afternoons there, sharing chili cheese fries, vanilla milkshakes, and gossiping about boys.

Across the street was Chip's Hardware in a line of old brick buildings, crumbling from deferred maintenance. Chip gave Adrian her first job. It wasn't glamorous like Laura's job at The Twistee Freeze, but it certainly taught her a lot. Chip had insisted on showing Adrian a thing or two when it was slow in the shop, and she owed her minimal handiness to him. So much of her old stomping grounds were exactly the same, except several old storefronts were boarded up, with slightly askew For Lease signs hanging in the windows.

The vision of Margaret dying haunted Adrian, assuring her she was doing the right thing. No one deserved to die alone, regardless of wounds from the past floating to the surface with their recent reunion. Adrian remembered her mother instilling in her at a young age the importance of being the bigger person when in an argument and apologizing first. She never thought she'd have to be the bigger person with her own mother, but three years was long enough. Continuing to let their differences come between them just didn't feel right. Maybe once they had a chance to spend time together, it would help them move forward and let the past drift away in favor of new, albeit short-term, memories.

Adrian turned into Shady Acres, the retirement community her mother moved to right before they'd stopped talking. Retirement communities were always akin to God's waiting room in Adrian's mind. She'd read an article recently about the rise of sexually transmitted diseases in places like that, with old people hyped up on little blue pills trying desperately to recapture any semblance of their youth. She shuddered at the thought.

At least the community was well maintained. She passed

several enclaves of houses with fancy names like "Gardenia Villas" and "Honeysuckle Cottages." There were two sidewalks: one designated for walking and the other for golf carts. The landscaping was meticulously manicured. It reminded her of Stepford, or at least a version of Stepford designated for the dying.

As she navigated her way around the Blue Heron golf course, she turned into her mother's subdivision. The homes were charming despite their ticky-tacky uniformity. They all had at least one sago palm tree in the front yard and stucco exteriors in varying shades of beige, butter cream, sage, and white. Adrian silently thanked whomever invented GPS, since looking for the white house on the left would have done her no good.

She hit the brakes a little too hard when the GPS signaled arrival at the destination. Her pulse raced as she parked, the pounding in her ears drowning out the hum of her idle engine. *Time to rip the Band-Aid off*. She killed the engine and walked around to the trunk. She retrieved one of her suitcases and slung her backpack over one shoulder, leaving the rest for whenever she needed a brief reprieve from her mother. The wheels of her suitcase clicked over the stone pavers as she ascended the driveway. Margaret opened the door before Adrian could knock. Adrian's heart sank.

It's worse than I thought.

———

"Oh, I didn't realize you were here already," Margaret said.

It had only been a few months since Adrian last saw her mother, but she wasn't falling for Margaret's poor attempts to hide obvious signs of health deterioration. She looked thinner, her face poorly under her makeup, and bags hung heavy under her eyes. She wore a white collared shirt with a faint coffee stain on the chest and peered at Adrian through drug store readers.

Adrian didn't dare comment, suddenly feeling six years old again, fearing retaliation for stepping out of line. Instead, "Just pulled up," were the only words she squeaked out.

Adrian attempted to end the awkwardness by leaning in for a hug. Margaret reciprocated with two swift pats on the back before pulling away. They stood awkwardly, unsure of how to fill the void.

Margaret pointed to her mailbox at the end of the driveway. "I was just going to check the mail."

"I'll take these things inside." Adrian moved out of the way.

"Your room is the second door on the left down the hall."

Adrian watched her mother get the mail, khakis threatening to slide off her body. Maybe she would have an easier time if she had a cane. Adrian knew better than to bring that up to Margaret. A woman who epitomized keeping up appearances, Margaret wouldn't be caught dead looking old, even if it did make things easier for her.

Adrian carried her things across the threshold, gaining familiarity with her surroundings. A galley kitchen, closed off from the living room, was to the right. It was clean and modest, with cream-colored Formica countertops and pickled oak cabinets reminiscent of a certain stomachache reliever. A round chestnut table and matching chairs filled the small dining room beyond the kitchen. A bay window provided a view of what the neighbors were up to. The television recounted local nefarious activity via a local news station. The set was framed by a worn recliner and small sofa in the living room straight ahead.

Adrian descended a hallway to her left, passing a bathroom decorated with a white frilly shower curtain and powder blue walls before finding her bedroom. The room reminded her of her teenage bedroom, except posters of New Kids on the Block and Mario Lopez weren't taped haphazardly to the walls. A sage green quilt covered a queen-sized bed against the wall, with four pillows propped artistically against the brass headboard. A white oak nightstand leaned against the bed frame, adorned by a modest lamp emitting a warm glow underneath its neutral lamp shade. To the right of the bed were white folding doors enclosing the contents of a closet. Against the wall at the foot of the bed stood a small white oak dresser embellished with a lace doily and a few pictures in small frames. Adrian dropped her suitcase by the closet and went to look at the three pictures: one of her parents on the beach at sunset, one of Adrian and Brad taken about three months after they started dating, and another one of Adrian and Laura from prom night. She wondered if her mother strategically placed the photos there in honor of her arrival.

Adrian jumped when she heard the screen door slam. Margaret had a hard time catching her breath, coughing as she shuffled into the living room. The bittersweetness of their new role-reversal reality sank in. Was Adrian up for the challenge?

Her mother coughed with more force. *Maybe she needs water.*

After searching the kitchen for glasses and filling one with water, Adrian took it to her mother. Margaret took healthy gulps, her hand shaking as she set the half-full glass down on the metal-framed table next to her dark blue recliner. "You didn't have to do that."

"It's no problem," Adrian muttered, sitting down on the beige sofa. The hum of the TV filled the void between them. It was nestled between two built-in bookshelves against the wall, tastefully spruced up with picture frames and knick-knacks. French doors allowed for natural light from a small patio in the backyard. Margaret's bedroom must be down the hall to the right. Adrian stole glances at her mother, watching her chest rise and fall as she breathed.

"I didn't realize the casual, no makeup look was in vogue," Margaret said.

"I didn't realize formal attire was required to visit." Adrian folded her arms across her chest.

"You never know who you might run into."

"I was in my car most of the time. You know, driving...to get here. I didn't really stop and socialize on the way."

"Are we not socializing now?"

"I stand corrected." Adrian raised her hands in defeat. "I'm so glad I'm here, and thanks for the warm welcome. What can I do for you?"

Margaret sighed. "Don't treat me like a sick old lady, and don't baby me."

"No problem."

Margaret turned her attention back to the television, signifying the end of that conversation. Adrian felt out of body, questioning her new reality. Could she handle living with her mother again? When she looked at Margaret, the resounding answer had to be yes. She could still see the image of her dying. Regardless of the pain caused by both of them in the past, she had to do the right thing. She'd suppress her urge to run out the front door and never look back.

So much had changed in the last three years. Adrian never had the courage to come out and ask why her mother hadn't told her sooner about her father's health. She kept waiting for her to apologize and offer an explanation, but one never came. She felt the living room shrink, the elephant closing in on them.

"I'm sorry about Brad." Margaret didn't break her gaze from the drama on the screen. Was the elephant suffocating her too?

"It's okay. It's not anyone's fault." Adrian wanted to believe that statement. Part of her did but the other felt guilty. She'd replayed their last months together in her mind, searching for anything she could have done differently to cause a different outcome. Maybe if she'd been more supportive or encouraging or less baby crazed. Maybe if she'd given him more, he wouldn't have cheated. He'd still be alive.

But would they be happy?

"At the risk of sounding callous, I think your life is better without him."

And there it was. In such a swift statement, Margaret reopened old wounds Adrian had spent years trying to heal. And she'd thought maybe her mother was about to apologize for not telling her sooner about her father. But instead, she decided to assert her opinion where it wasn't wanted. Adrian remembered when Margaret told her at her father's funeral that she thought Adrian was making a big mistake marrying Brad. Adrian wouldn't dare give her mother the satisfaction of knowing the truth—that her marriage was, in fact, not perfect. She'd rather carry that one to her grave.

"I think I'm going to take a walk." Adrian needed to get out of there.

"I don't mean to hurt your feelings, but I—"

"Not now." Adrian put up her hand to stop her mother from saying more. She walked out the front door, letting it slam behind her. She looked up and down the street, realizing the very real possibility of getting lost in the uniformity. She felt lost already, conflicting emotions that she'd spent years suppressing bubbling to the surface. If one stupid comment from her mother pinched a nerve, she obviously wasn't ready to face them. There were only two things she needed in that moment: to talk to her best friend and a cigarette.

She pulled out her cell phone and dialed Laura's number. While the phone rang, she retrieved the pack of cigarettes from her car to help take the edge off the whole situation. Laura answered. "How's everything going?"

"Not so great." Adrian took a long drag. "She insulted me for not wearing a formal gown and tiara for my arrival, and she already told me she still thinks Brad was an idiot."

"She really said that?"

"No, I'm exaggerating a little. But she might as well have."

"Give it some time. You've only been there for how long now?"

"Like an hour or something." It sure felt like a lot longer.

"This isn't going to be easy, and not many people would do what you're doing. Be proud of that."

"You're right, although now I'm tempted to put her in a home."

Laura chuckled. "Hang in there. Things will get easier. Actually, now that I think of it, my yoga instructor shared something with us at the end of our last class that may help you in this situation."

Laura has always been the yin to Adrian's yang, the hippy-dippy to her practicality. She wondered what words of wisdom from a hipster-yogi could possibly apply to her situation, but anything was worth a shot. "Hit me with it."

"She gave us the mantra of *peace begins with me* to repeat throughout our day. I think you should try it."

"Peace begins with me," Adrian repeated. She felt

herself relax slightly. Maybe Laura was onto something. "Okay, I'll give it a try."

"Do I smell smoke?" Margaret asked, opening the front door.

Busted.

Adrian felt seventeen again, quickly putting out the evidence. "I gotta go." She hung up and looked at her mother, who towered over her, making her suddenly feel small.

"Honestly, Adrian, if you feel like smoking, just look at me. All of this could be your future." Margaret waved her hands over her body like a geriatric Vanna White.

"I wasn't smoking." Adrian avoided eye contact.

Margaret scoffed. "You're just like your father—a terrible liar."

"I'm going to go unpack," Adrian mumbled. She went straight to her bedroom to avoid any further lecturing. *Peace begins with me. Peace begins with me.*

8

Adrian woke up startled, taking a few moments to realize where she was. Even after a couple of weeks, she still hadn't gotten used to waking up in her mother's house. She couldn't hear the TV, so she must have woken up before Margaret.

Her bare feet retracted from the cold tile before sliding into her slippers. She trudged toward the kitchen in search of her daily fix. She needed caffeine and needed it bad. She turned on the coffeepot, and while it percolated, she quietly fixed breakfast for her mother.

"Good morning." Margaret rubbed her eyes as she walked into the kitchen, her pink bathrobe tied tightly around her waist.

"Breakfast is almost ready." Adrian spooned cottage cheese onto a plate with half a grapefruit.

Margaret sat at the dining table and looked out the bay window. Adrian brought her coffee and breakfast, happy to see she'd grabbed the pill box containing her morning meds. Adrian joined her at the table with a cup of coffee and they sipped in silence. The morning fog began to dissipate, revealing dew-kissed grass shimmering in the emerging sunlight.

"Aren't you going to eat?" Margaret asked.

"In a minute. I need coffee first." Adrian warmed her hands against the steaming mug.

"You need to eat. You're too skinny. No man likes a woman who is too skinny," Margaret mumbled through bites of cottage cheese.

"Joe is all the man I need." Adrian sipped appreciatively.

Margaret shook her head. "You're too young to be giving up."

"I'm not giving up. I'm still mourning."

"Brad wasn't—"

Adrian put up her hand. "Eat your breakfast."

They sat in silence as Margaret finished. "So, what are you going to do?"

"I just said I'm not concerned about dating."

"Not about that, silly. What are you going to do with yourself? Don't you need a job or something?"

Adrian hadn't thought about work lately, for the first time in her adult life. Between her severance package and what was left from the small life insurance policy for Brad, she wasn't exactly desperate for money. She knew it wouldn't last forever, but the idea of going back to the rat race of corporate America made her stomach curdle. The one thing she always wanted to do and never explored was painting. She remembered enjoying it when she was younger, until her mother said her father was the artist of the family. She'd folded up her easel in pursuit of climbing the corporate ladder, hoping to win her mother's approval. "I think I'd like to paint."

Margaret rolled her eyes. "That's not exactly going to pay the bills."

"I don't need to worry about that right now."

"Whatever money you have saved will run out eventually. Think about that before you become unemployable."

"Is there a craft store nearby?" Maybe she could set up a small easel in her room or take one to the beach.

"You're serious about painting?" When Adrian nodded, Margaret sighed. "Well, there's a craft store out on route 99..." she trailed off, looking out the window. Her eyes bugged out of her head, and she turned to Adrian. "How do I look?"

"Fine?"

Margaret combed her fingers through her short hair and wrapped the bathrobe even tighter. "It's Harold." Adrian gave her a confused look. "Just answer the door."

The doorbell rang, and Adrian answered. A man who looked to be in his early 70s greeted her. He was a couple of inches shorter than her, with a panama jack pulled low to obscure his vision. "You're not Margaret." He tilted his head to see Adrian. He looked like a quintessential Floridian in his Tommy Bahama shirt with one too many buttons undone, showing a hemp necklace nestled in the salt and pepper forest on his chest. He held an opaque jar labeled Coconut Oil.

"I'm her daughter, Adrian. And you are?"

"Harold," Margaret cooed, pushing Adrian to the side.

"There you are." He beamed. "You look radiant."

Margaret giggled. Was she blushing?

"I brought you the oil, just as you requested."

"You are such a sweetheart. Thank you." Margaret reached for the jar. Their hands touched, lingering as they locked eyes. Perma-grins spread across their faces. "Let me get my purse. How much do I owe you?"

"The usual is fine, as long as you save me some of whatever you're making with it." He rocked back and forth on the balls of his feet.

"I think I can manage that." Margaret winked, handing the jar to Adrian while she grabbed her wallet. She took out two twenty-dollar bills and gave them to Harold.

"Thank you, Margaret," he said, their gazes locked on one another.

"I should have some leftovers on Friday if you want to stop by then."

"I wouldn't miss it. I'll see you then." He smiled and turned to walk away.

"Thank you, Harold," she said, her voice coated in honey. She slowly closed the door but left it open just a crack to watch Harold turn around and tip his hat to her before she closed it completely. When she turned around, there was a dreamy look in her eye.

"Since when is coconut oil so expensive?"

Margaret's expression changed, the dream fading. "It's not."

"Then why was this $40?" Adrian examined the jar.

"Convenience."

"That's a hell of a convenience charge."

"That's basic supply and demand." Margaret took the jar out of her hands and put it on a shelf in the pantry in the kitchen. "I'm having the girls over Thursday evening."

"That sounds like fun." Adrian had heard about her mother's friends, Gilda and Bev, but hadn't had a chance to meet them yet. When Margaret didn't offer more detail, she wondered if it was her mother's way of asking her to make other plans. "Do you not want me to be here?"

"Oh, I...guess that would be fine."

"If you don't want me to be here..."

"No, you're welcome to join. I just hope we're not too boring for you is all." Margaret picked an invisible piece of lint from her shirt.

"I'd love to meet your friends." Adrian smiled.

Margaret nodded in acceptance.

Adrian rinsed dishes in the sink. "So, Harold seems really nice."

"He is." Margaret volunteered nothing more. Adrian looked at her expectantly, but her mother's lips were sealed. "Anything else?"

"No, I guess I'll finish this up and go check out that art store on 99."

"Good, I'm going to watch the news." Margaret settled into her recliner.

"Didn't you used to tell me TV would rot my brain?"

"Shh...I'm busy."

Adrian left her alone with the talking heads, still wondering about the price of coconut oil.

———

ADRIAN PARKED in public access parking across from the beach. She decided to take her new art supplies down near the water. What better subject to work on than the peaceful beauty of the beach? It would also give her a break from her mother.

She lugged her backing board and supplies like a pack mule, feeling the sand slip between her toes as she found a place to set up shop. She took a deep breath, tasting the salty air on her tongue as she admired the natural beauty of ebb and flow. Two older women power walked along the shore, and a little boy built a sandcastle with his father while mom stayed safely planted underneath an oversized umbrella, lost in a book. A couple of kids splashed in the water, and teenagers attempted to surf the non-existent waves.

Adrian focused her attention on the family building a castle, deciding they could be the subject of her maiden art voyage. She got everything prepped, taping a piece of watercolor paper to her backing board and pouring clean water from a bottle into two separate jars. She pulled out her new brushes and opened her watercolor pan set.

Where to start?

Maybe she needed to draft in pencil first.

Resolved, she traded her brush for a pencil. She looked at the family scene in front of her, ready to recreate the magic. But her hands were cement, unable to reach the paper.

Adrian always had a natural eye and talent when it came to art. She even received an Arbor Day Art Award for her painting of a palm tree in the third grade. Her father had beamed with pride, knowing he'd gifted Adrian with the ability to capture the natural beauty in her surroundings. Instead of congratulating her, Margaret's expression soured. *Your father is the artist in the family*. Her mother's words paralyzed her then, and they still did.

But she was wrong, wasn't she?

Adrian wished that her father was still alive, able to provide words of wisdom and encouragement in the moment. She felt tears form in her eyes and realized she was still angry at her mother for robbing her the chance to say goodbye to the most important man in her life. "Dad, I need your help," she said to the wind. She wiped her eyes, questioning her sanity when she waited for a response.

It's just paint, a small voice squeaked in her mind. Startled, she wondered if she'd imagined the voice. *You got this*, it said.

"Dad?"

What would make him proud?

Adrian pondered the question, polishing it in her mind. Then it hit her. She knew exactly what she needed to do.

She grabbed a pencil, quickly marking rough sketches

on her paper. At times, her hands didn't feel like her own, like some force outside of herself were guiding the pencil over the paper. She trusted it more than herself at that point, whatever it was.

When her hand stopped, she admired how the sketch perfectly captured her vision. Seagulls cawed overhead as she glanced once more at the family portrait by the shoreline. *This is much more beautiful.*

She picked up her paint pans, ready to bring the sketch to life. She held her breath before the brush hit paper for the first time.

The scariest part is right before you start, the voice said to her.

She took a deep breath and made contact, sweeping the brush in one long, radiant light-yellow stroke. There. The first step was done, and it wasn't as scary as she thought. Something flickered to life in her with that first stroke. It was what she was meant to do all along. She wasn't meant for boardrooms or wool suits anymore. She was meant to bask in the glory of God's creation, doing her best to recreate its beauty one stroke at a time. She'd opened Pandora's pochade box and refused to ever close it again.

As her heart burst into artistic flames, she wielded her hands to merge Heaven and Earth on her paper canvas for the rest of the afternoon.

———

MARGARET SAT at her dining table rubbing her eyes after waking from a three-hour nap. She lacked the energy or desire to eat. She'd always had a good appetite, and when that started to change, she knew something was wrong. Although she still had plenty of fight in her, even if her body was slowly dying.

Her doctor said it would happen. He said it along with words and phrases like *progressive,* and *treatment would help with the pain*, and *need to start immediately*. She'd only heard half of what he said and comprehended less. She didn't need to hear every word to get the gist.

When she decided to forgo treatment, her doctor had other words to say, like *didn't advise* and *should she change her mind*. But she wouldn't. She knew as soon as she heard *stage four*, it was over. She didn't want to put anyone through the pain of watching her die slowly, with treatment only delaying the inevitable. She intended to die with dignity or at least with as much as she could, given her body would soon betray her.

She took pride in being self-sufficient, a pillar of strength for those around her when they needed a boost. God's sense of humor wasn't lost on her. Now she was the one who needed a pillar of strength to lean on.

"Maybe it's time to call Adrian," Gilda had said to her. Gilda and Bev, being cancer survivors themselves, knew immediately what was going on with Margaret without her uttering a word. Maybe Margaret wasn't as good as she thought at hiding the truth.

Margaret didn't have the fight in her any longer to disagree, but she didn't want the C-word to be the reason she and her daughter reconciled their differences. And when Adrian said she would come, Margaret had a hard time accepting it. She'd never been able to ask anyone for help in her sixty-something years alive, so what was the point now? Besides, there was a part of her that believed if she voiced her need for help out loud it would be her death sentence. Not that cancer was being kind to her regardless. She fully expected its retribution to be cruel and, God willing, swift.

She hadn't prayed in a long time but had recently

reopened her channels of communication with God. She imagined Him in His white robe and olive branch crown, stroking a thick white beard while He considered how to handle her cries for mercy. She'd turned her back on God years earlier, feeling a sense of betrayal from one of His missionaries in the church. She'd struggled after Adrian was born with what people had since started calling postpartum depression, and she didn't think she'd survive another pregnancy. She went to the priest seeking counsel on the matter, wanting approval to use birth control to avoid going through the pain she'd endured. He reminded her that using birth control was considered a sin and encouraged her to rely on the rhythm method instead. It was a fatal blow to her relationship with God, and she decided to rely on modern medical advancements anyway and slowly stopped going to church.

Her separation from the church drove a wedge between her and some of her closest friends and even caused tension with George. But she didn't have a choice—it was life and death for her, and she chose to live in spite of disapproval.

Now she was staring death in the face, reaching her hand out for the God she'd turned her back on years ago. She longed to feel His fingers entwine with hers, lovingly shepherding her to the next phase of her journey. She'd recently pulled out her rosary from the jewelry box and wore it as a reminder to stay close to Him during the treacherous time. Her mind guffawed the first time she wore it, chiding her for being a complete phony. But what did she know anyway? She didn't imagine God to be as unforgiving as her mind. It was one of the few thoughts that kept her going.

Her fingers brushed the hematite beads of the rosary while she struggled with the weight of her eyelids. She'd better lie down again before the excitement later with the girls. It would be the first time she'd invited her daughter to get a glimpse of who she was as a woman, not just as a mother, and it would be lying to say she didn't feel nervous. Knowing her friends, Margaret hoped to still have a daughter after the evening's get-together.

9

After reaching a stopping point, Adrian decided to let the paint dry before finishing her portrait. She packed up her supplies and carried them back to the car, careful not to touch anything with the ends of her slightly damp painting. Despite it being a winter day, the sun still beat down, bringing the temperature to the manageable low 70s. Adrian had to admit, she had missed winter in Florida. It was a welcome reprieve from recent rainy winters in Austin.

She gingerly opened the back door of the sedan and placed the painting supplies on the floorboard, laying her work in progress on a towel across the back seat. Satisfied, she closed the door and turned to catch another glimpse of the shoreline a hundred yards away. But something else caught her eye.

She saw a small group of people gathering, some of them holding small cups of coffee from a portable carafe sitting on a nearby folding table. A white sign with red letters, "Bereaved by the Beach," leaned against the table, a red arrow pointing their direction. She'd considered group therapy when she and Brad were having fertility issues, having read stories about how helpful it was just to be heard by others who truly understood their strife. If Adrian were being honest, she'd carried quite a burden in the past few months: infertility, infidelity, and death, both literally and figuratively. Maybe this was a sign. Maybe she could use a shoulder of someone who could help her make sense of the recent losses.

Adrian assessed her appearance: paint-stained hands and soft, loose clothing. She touched the top of her head, feeling the ridges and bumps of hair on top of her less-than-perfect ponytail. She didn't have a lick of makeup on either, but at least she'd brushed her teeth. Maybe she should return when she wasn't so disheveled.

Go, a voice said to her.

Lacking complete cognitive control over her movements, Adrian realized she'd locked her car and walked toward the group. She wasn't perfect, but it didn't matter. She was in all her non-glory. Group therapy was supposed to be a judgment-free zone anyway, right?

Her pulse raced as she approached the table, hands shaky as she pushed the lever to dispense coffee into a paper cup. The warm contents in her cold hands provided some comfort as she took a sip to calm her nerves. She saw a woman with a blond bob approach in her periphery.

"Hi, I'm Karen. I don't think we've met," she said. Her green eyes were as warm and inviting as the tender timber of her voice, and Adrian felt herself relax slightly.

"No, we haven't. I'm Adrian." She held out her left hand for Karen to shake, pulling it away after seeing the stains under her fingernails. "Sorry about my hands."

Karen brushed off her apology with a wave of her hand. "So, are you...?"

"Bereaved?"

Karen chuckled nervously. "Yes, there isn't an easy way to ask, huh?"

Adrian nodded, pushing a strand of hair behind her ear.

"Well, we're about to start if you'd like to stay. You can share with us whenever you're ready, or if you just want to listen, that's fine too. No pressure."

"Yeah, I'd like that." The words fell out of Adrian's mouth. She wondered who or what possessed her, feeling out of body as she settled into a folding chair in a circle underneath the pavilion.

She nodded and said hello to the four other people in the circle, who introduced themselves as Frank, Henry, Gina and Susan. Everyone seemed normal, their smiles warm despite the heavy burden they shared behind their eyes. Adrian felt her body relax more. For the first time in months, she didn't feel so alone. The people at the meeting had stories to share of their own, stories of love and loss. But they'd carried on, and so could she.

"Sorry I'm late." A man in a crisp charcoal suit and red tie took a seat next to Adrian. She stole glances at the newcomer from her periphery. He had a familiarity she couldn't put her finger on. His dark curly hair and deep brown eyes made her heart stop. The wood, orange and ginseng notes of his cologne tickled her senses. Maybe she didn't know him, but she definitely wanted to.

"Glad you made it, Christian," Karen said.

Christian. Why did that sound familiar?

"Okay, thank you all for coming." Karen drew Adrian's attention back to the present. "Today we'll be dealing with the F-word."

What kind of therapy was this?

"Forgiveness!" Karen chuckled. "Forgiveness is one of the greatest challenges we face as we try to process a new reality without our loved ones. The grief we feel from their passing is normal, and forgiveness can feel unnatural. But in order for our hearts to heal, we need to face this F-word. Does anyone have something they'd like to share about forgiveness?"

The group was silent for a beat before a woman across from Adrian cleared her throat. "I guess I'll go." She shifted her heavy body in the small chair, pushing brown hair behind her right ear.

"Here we go," Susan mumbled under her breath, punctuated by an eyeroll.

"Hi. I'm Gina, and as some of you may know, I lost my daughter, Trudy, in a car accident." She paused, holding her breath to keep tears from forming in the corners of her brown eyes. "Trudy was only seven. She would have been eight next Thursday."

Karen passed Gina a box of tissues, and Gina thanked her as she pulled out a white square and balled it in her fist. "I've replayed the accident over in my mind countless times, and every time, I can only blame myself."

"But you know it's not your fault," Adrian said. "Sometimes a car, or a semi, comes out of nowhere." She crossed her arms over her chest, shrinking under the intense gaze from the group.

"You're right, but my problem is I'd been sending a text to one of the other gymnastics moms, saying we were running late. I should have let Steve drive. He knew I was distracted and hated feeling rushed. I looked down one moment to send that stupid text and the next, we were crashing into a car, my whole life gone in a flash."

"You're still here, aren't you?" Susan said. "You can't say your life is gone."

"What happened to your husband?" Adrian asked.

"Well, he survived. Barely. But we didn't." Gina dabbed her face with the tissue. "We drifted apart about six months after Trudy died. I guess we reminded each other too much of what we'd lost. That and I didn't always look this way." She gestured to her round figure. "I'm not sure how I can ever forgive myself for—" Her voice cracked, and she seemed unable to say more.

Karen reached over and rubbed Gina's back. "It's okay. Let it out."

"I wish I could go back and tell myself to let Steve drive or not send that text, or—"

"Put down the cake?" Frank said. Susan giggled.

Gina's eyes bulged. "Yes, that too, Frank." She laughed nervously, breaking the tension in the group.

"Honey, you know I love you." Frank blew her a kiss. "But you gotta stop blaming yourself for this. Look at what it's done to you."

"I know." Gina sniffled.

"It's not healthy," Frank added.

"Frank's right," Karen said.

"I mean, at least you had a daughter." Adrian said. "Some people never get that chance."

Christian shifted in his chair next to Adrian.

"Tell me more about Trudy," Adrian said.

"Trudy was my mini-me," Gina said. "But she was full of beans, very charismatic, and didn't know a stranger. She got that from Steve. She would go up to people and just sing to them. One time, I found her surrounded by neighbors as she sang them Christmas carols. In August, no less." She giggled. "Everyone was in total awe of her everywhere she went. She had a pure heart, a big toothy smile, and it was hard to stay mad at her. I was so proud to be her momma. Still am, I guess."

"Just because your child is gone doesn't mean you're not a mom anymore," Karen said.

"Or a woman," Frank added.

"Frank's right, honey," Henry said. Adrian would have thought Henry was in his 40s had it not been for his white hair. His smooth cocoa skin barely had any signs of age. "Trudy wouldn't want this for her momma."

"I've been going to yoga three times a week. Do you want to join me?" Karen asked.

"I think that would be nice. Thank you." Gina smiled at Karen.

As the group expressed words of encouragement to Gina, Adrian imagined Trudy in her mind from Gina's description. She could see her vividly, crossing over into Heaven and being greeted by the little girl as they chased each other through the daffodils, laughing until their sides hurt. She felt compelled to bring the vision into their reality, perhaps even share it with Gina. Maybe she would at the next meeting.

Was she already committing to next time?

"Anyone else have something they'd like to share? Adrian?" Karen said.

Adrian shook her head.

"Okay, well, let's talk a moment about the word forgiveness. For some, this can trigger anger or resentment toward the person we lost or ourselves. Does that resonate with anyone?"

"Yeah, I'm angry," Adrian said. "In fact, I'm angry at my husband and myself." Her eyebrows raised. She'd surprised herself with the honesty in front of strangers. "How could I be so stupid to ignore the signs that he was cheating? Then he goes and dies, almost taking me with him, and everyone is like, 'Oh, Brad was such a great husband,' and 'Oh, what a huge loss. You must be devastated.' What a bunch of crap. What about me? I wish someone would tell me how stupid I am. How I was so baby-crazed I missed my marriage falling apart. And now he's some kind of martyr, and I'm left to pick up the pieces."

"Okay, you're stupid," Frank said. "But I was stupid too. Grant cheated on me, contracted HIV, and I was left with the impossible choice of taking care of him while he died or deserting him when he needed someone the most. That last year was hard."

"Are you...?" Adrian asked.

"Positive? No, we hadn't slept together in months," Frank said. "It's hard to take off the rose-colored glasses when it comes to those we love or once loved. I was blind to the issues we had too."

"You're a better person than me, I guess," Adrian said.

"No, I'm not." Frank leaned forward in his chair. "I realized that Grant would die, and I'd have to live with the consequences of what I did or didn't do. I decided to be the bigger person. I wanted to leave and run so many times, but I couldn't. My momma raised me better than that."

Adrian paused. "How did you make peace with it all?"

"I'll tell you when I do," Frank said.

"That's why we're all here, hon," Henry said.

"You're not alone," Karen said. Others nodded in agreement.

Adrian looked around at the group of people who were vastly different but shared a common thread that held them together. She felt a weight lift off her chest. "Thank you." She held her breath, willing herself not to cry from the relief of being honest. Being real. She felt one step closer to healing, although she still had a long way to go.

After the meeting broke, Adrian stopped by the carafe to refill her small cup of coffee. Christian approached her, grabbing a cup for himself.

"Adrian Russo," he said.

"Foley now." She turned to look at him, his hazel eyes piercing her heart. Her breath caught in her throat.

"It's been a long time." He dusted his coffee with powdered creamer.

"Yeah, I guess it has..." She trailed off. She felt rude not being able to place him, as he was definitely someone she shouldn't forget.

"You don't remember me, do you?" He smiled and his teeth were perfectly straight.

She grimaced. "Honestly, no. Sorry."

"It's okay. Not many people do. I've changed a lot in the last few years. I'm Christian...Stephens."

The Christian Stephens Adrian remembered was skinny as a rail with coke bottle glasses. Nothing like the man standing in front of her. His broad shoulders perfectly filled out his blazer, and she could see his defined pecs peeking through a white collared shirt. "Wow, you look...different." Could she be any less eloquent?

"And you are just as I remember." He smiled.

They locked eyes, and Adrian's skin prickled with electricity.

"Hey, Adrian," Karen said. "Thanks for being brave today." She squeezed Adrian's shoulder. "We'll see you next week?"

"Yes, I'll be here." She didn't take her eyes from Christian's.

Christian's phone rang, and Karen left to talk to Henry. "I gotta take this, but it was great seeing you again," he said. "Sounds like I'll see you next week?"

"Yeah, I wouldn't miss you. I mean, miss it." *Oh Lord*. Her face flushed.

He smiled and answered the phone. She heard a high-pitched female voice on the other end, babbling. She watched Christian walk away, and he turned to look at her one more time before rounding the corner toward his car.

She'd known the odds of running into an old classmate were high when she moved back. She never would have guessed she'd have a reunion at group therapy and never suspected Christian would have turned out the way he did. She wondered about his story, seeing the same thread of pain in his eyes when they looked at one another.

Which, in all honesty, she wanted to keep doing. That caught her by surprise. The dirt on Brad's grave had barely settled. Could she even entertain the idea of moving on? But it wasn't like she would have predicted her life to make the twists and turns it had recently, and at some point, she needed to move on.

And to her relief, she didn't need to figure it all out right then.

If the last few months had taught her anything, it was to expect the unexpected, and she silently thanked the Universe for making her first reunion with a former class-mate surprisingly good.

————

"OH SHOOT. I just realized what day it was and you're prob-ably at group," Bev said when Christian answered.

"No, your timing is fine. We just finished. What's up?"

"I was calling to let you know I can't do dinner tonight. Margie is having us girls over to her place."

Christian had a standing appointment with his aunt Bev every Thursday after group therapy for dinner. He'd started the tradition after his uncle Jim died two years before. He did his best to stave off Bev's loneliness as much as possible.

"Oh, that's okay. I'll just pick up a pizza or something." Christian hadn't realized how much he'd looked forward to their weekly dinners too. Sometimes the emptiness of his apartment hit him hard, especially after group.

"You sure you're okay?"

"Yeah, I'm fine." He cleared his throat as he unlocked the car and slid into the driver's seat. "What's the occasion?"

"Her daughter just moved back. You remember Adrian, don't you?"

Oh, he definitely did. Seeing Adrian had caught him completely off-guard. She looked exactly like he remembered her, a beautiful blast from his past.

"Christian?"

"Sorry, cutting over to Bluetooth." He scrambled to turn on the car. "Yeah, I just ran into her actually."

"Where? At group?"

"Yeah, she was sitting in the circle when I arrived." And sitting next to her did nothing to help his concentration, but he decided to keep that to himself.

"Well?"

"Well, what?" he replied.

"Did you talk to her?"

"Yeah, I told her it was nice to see her again." Which was true but also a severe understatement.

"I like the sound of this."

"I didn't say anything."

"You don't have to."

Christian sighed. "Anything else?"

"Yeah, don't go back to work tonight because we're not having dinner. Life's too short to work as hard as you do."

She knew him far too well. He had already planned on heading back to catch up on his paperwork and prepare for court on Friday. After all, that's what Uncle Jim would have done if he were still there. "Okay, Auntie. Have a good time tonight with the girls."

"I will, and I'll put in a good word for you with you-know-who."

"That's not—"

"Bye!" She hung up.

He couldn't help but chuckle at his aunt's behavior. Who needed a dating website or matchmaker when there was Aunt Bev? Seeing Adrian had been a defibrillator for his dormant heart, and he felt sick with nerves when she smiled at him. Maybe he actually stood a chance? He certainly wasn't an awkward teenager anymore.

Not that he was ready to date after what had happened.

He pulled into a parking spot to pick up dinner from Sal's, his favorite pizza place. Adrian's image flashed in his mind. He considered the possibility of being shirtless in front of a woman again in the relative near future and thought he'd better skip the pizza. Even if the opportunity presented itself, was he ready for it? There hadn't been anyone since Sarah. After what she did to him, he'd put his heart in a box on a shelf for safe keeping, vowing to never let a woman hurt him that way again.

But Adrian wasn't just anyone. She was the it-girl, the one he'd pined after for years in high school but never mustered up enough courage to do anything about it. It seemed like the Universe was conspiring in his favor, giving him an opportunity to do things differently the next time around. He'd grown and changed quite a bit since then, and he wanted to discover how Adrian had changed too.

After ordering a salad and baked ziti to go, he headed toward home, considering how he would handle the second chance with his dream girl.

10

―――――

"Do you need help with that?" Adrian asked.

"No, I've got it," Margaret said. She took a pan of brownies out of the oven. Their rich, intoxicating smell wafted through the kitchen. "They should be here any minute."

"Are you sure you don't mind me staying?"

"No, it's fine." Margaret pushed a loose strand of hair away from her face. "As long as you don't mind hanging out with three old broads."

"I'd love to meet your friends."

Adrian set the table for four, each place setting flanked by water and wine glasses, while Margaret turned the television to a jazz standards music station. Adrian felt relieved to hear Old Blue-Eyes croon about the moon instead of the angry chatter from the news.

"So, what do you typically do when they come over?"

"We play cards and gossip." Margaret smiled. "We usually try out new recipes. They know how much I like to bake, so they leave me in charge of dessert."

"Sounds good to me." Adrian's stomach growled, and

she eyed the brownies while she considered skipping straight to dessert.

The doorbell rang, and Margaret greeted her girlfriends warmly. As they crossed the threshold, Adrian knew immediately who was who. Gilda, a tall, lanky redhead with a short bob reminiscent of a flapper, held a bowl of chicken pesto pasta in her arms with a navy towel wrapped around it to keep it warm. Bev, a short, stocky brunette wearing a blue knitted cap and a heavy charcoal cardigan that was overkill for temperatures in the 70s, held a salad bowl with a loaf of French bread on top. Just like her mother, Margaret's friends were obviously still concerned with their appearances. They both still dyed their hair—what was left of it anyway—and they both wore makeup, although Gilda had on significantly more than Bev.

"This must be Adrian," Gilda said. She reminded Adrian of a phoenix with her beak-like nose and dark beady eyes. "She's more beautiful than you lead on, Margie."

Adrian blushed. "Thank you." She took the salad from Bev and set it on the counter, and Gilda followed close behind with her pasta. "Does the pasta need to be heated up at all?"

"No, it should be fine as long as we're ready to eat."

Adrian nodded and started dishing out portions on her mother's white Corelle plates.

"Did you remember the...?" Margaret asked her friends, raising an eyebrow.

"Of course! It wouldn't be a dinner party without it." Gilda winked. "How are you holding up, Margie?" She placed a hand on Margaret's shoulder. "What did your doctor say about forgoing treatment? Has the cancer spread?"

"Spread?" Adrian dropped the tongs in the salad bowl. "No treatment? What is she talking about, Ma?"

The room grew eerily quiet except for Satchmo's trumpet in the background. "You haven't told her?" Bev asked, her mouth hanging open like a sea bass.

Margaret shook her head, looking down at the ground.

Gilda grimaced, apparently feeling like she'd done something she shouldn't have.

The proverbial pin dropped while Adrian waited for Margaret to say something. Anything. Maybe Gilda had her confused with someone else. Why would her mother choose to do nothing about her diagnosis? She'd always been a fighter. Why stop now? Worry, disappointment and anger swirled in her stomach. "Ma?"

"I guess you're going to find out eventually." Margaret gave Gilda a pointed look. "My cancer is aggressive, and I've decided not to do chemo or any other kind of treatment."

Bev reached out and touched Margaret's arm in a comforting way.

"Were you ever going to tell me?" Adrian felt nauseous with betrayal from hearing her mother's decision to give up. So many questions swirled around in her mind: How long did they have left? Why had Margaret kept Adrian in the dark? Was there any way she'd change her mind?

"Let's discuss this later. We have guests," Margaret said through a thin smile.

Adrian stared in disbelief. She really expected her to sweep it under the rug— pretend like it didn't exist? She might be able to do that but not Adrian.

Gilda mumbled an apology, and Margaret brushed it off, saying there was no need. "Adrian, do you mind plating our meals?" Her intense gaze said Adrian better drop the subject.

Adrian hesitated and then nodded. Her mother had instilled in her to never make a scene in public, and while they were at home, she didn't want to embarrass her mother in front of her friends. She knew how much Margaret's reputation meant to her, so Adrian decided to set it all aside until they were alone. But not before giving her a look meant to convey that it definitely wasn't the end of the conversation.

Adrian stayed quiet through the majority of the meal, pushing food from one side of her plate to another. She couldn't stop thinking about her mother's lack of fight, and the severity of the diagnosis. Margaret gave her a look out of the corner of her eye, one Adrian hadn't seen since she was a little girl. Adrian reluctantly took a bite, forcing herself to compartmentalize her thoughts and feelings while they had company.

She listened to the women gossip about people in the neighborhood, trying to keep up with their fast chatter and cast of characters. Adrian learned both Bev and Gilda were cancer survivors, with their respective breast and skin cancers thankfully in remission. Bev grew accustomed to knitting herself stylish hats while her hair regrew and couldn't shake the habit after she kicked the cancer. Gilda decided to keep her hair short, and said long hair just got in the way of everything. Adrian combed her fingers through her hair, thinking about Gilda's words. Her hair felt soft, and she really appreciated its length. She could put it up, leave it down, braid it...her thoughts trailed off as she realized conversation had come to a halt, with all eyes on her.

"I'd say it's working." Bev grinned. Gilda and Margaret nodded and giggled.

"What's working?" Adrian suddenly felt a little hazy.

"Honey, there's marijuana in everything we're eating," Gilda said, pulling her hands down from combing her hair.

Adrian's eyes grew wide as she eyed the pesto pasta and salad with an *herb* vinaigrette. Paranoia set in. "What if my mom finds out?"

"Too late," Margaret said. The three of them erupted with laughter.

"Margie, you didn't tell her?" Gilda asked between giggles, elbowing her friend playfully.

"Hey, she wanted to be included." Margaret shrugged and gave a goofy smile. "So, here we are."

"I can't believe you got me high." Adrian's jaw felt like it hit the floor. She knew her mother was capable of a lot but drugging her was unexpected.

"Lighten up, Adrian. Have a brownie." Margaret smiled, cutting into the pan to serve dessert.

"Are these...?"

Margaret nodded, reading her mind. "The oil from Harold."

Adrian couldn't believe it. Her mother was a pothead. And had a drug dealer. And pothead friends.

"Oh, Harold." Bev sighed. "You should totally hit that."

"Nah." Margaret brushed it off. "I raised a daughter, I buried a husband, I've lived my life." She had a slightly dreamy look in her eyes.

"Was he all googly-eyed when he dropped off the oil?" Gilda leaned toward Adrian.

"They both were!"

"Adrian!" Margaret admonished, and everyone laughed.

"Whatever. It's true."

Margaret stuck out her tongue at Adrian.

"What about you, dear?" Bev asked. "I heard you ran into my nephew today.

"Who's that?"

"Christian."

"Oh, yes. I did...but not literally." Adrian mimicked a run-in by slapping her hands together, giggling.

"No brownie for you, lightweight." Margaret took the brownie from Adrian.

Adrian slapped her mother's hand to leave it be, and Margaret drew it back in surprise. "I can hang," Adrian made a wave-like motion with her hand. When in Rome, right?

Gilda laughed. "Like mother, like daughter."

"Did he say anything about me?" Adrian asked.

"Not much. He played it cool," Bev said. "Although I know he had a thing for you back in high school." She winked.

"Really?" Adrian felt giddy, like she was seventeen again. Funny how time changed things. If she'd heard Christian had a thing for her back then, she wouldn't have given it a second thought. But hearing it now excited her.

"Yeah, but don't hold your breath." Margaret mumbled through a bite of brownie.

"What do you mean?"

"He's been gun shy ever since his ex cheated on him," Bev said.

"Yeah, I can relate. I mean, I can understand that." Adrian quickly corrected herself while Margaret raised an eyebrow at her.

"So, what about you and Christian, then?" Gilda asked.

"How did she put it? I buried a husband...I think I'm done?"

"Smart ass," Margaret said with a playful shove.

"You're too young to give up." Bev touched Adrian's hand. "Just give yourself some time."

"Alright, enough talk. Let's play cards." Margaret pushed back from the table to retrieve the deck of cards, handing them to Gilda.

"You in?" Gilda asked.

"Yeah, I'm already in this far, so why not?" Adrian shrugged. Gilda shuffled the cards and dealt everyone in for

Gin Rummy. While Adrian lost hand after hand, thoughts of Christian poked through her marijuana haze.

———

ADRIAN RUBBED the sleep from her eyes while she got dressed. Her mind worked overtime, still processing the things she'd learned at the previous night's dinner party (and perhaps still waiting for some of the buzz to wear off). Her mother, against her doctor's advice, wasn't undergoing any treatment for cancer. Adrian couldn't understand the logic or the lack of fight from a woman who was a perpetual fighter. Why was she giving up?

A light knock on the door interrupted her thoughts.

"Mind if I come in?" Margaret asked, poking her head through the doorway. Adrian nodded, and her mother barely entered the room, leaning against the wall near the doorway. "Going somewhere?"

"Just out."

"I take it you're mad at me." Margaret looked down at her feet.

"No, I'm not mad." Adrian pushed a loose strand of hair away from her face. "But I need you to be honest with me."

Margaret looked down, picking at an invisible piece of lint on her nightgown. "What do you want to know?"

"Why aren't you undergoing any kind of treatment?"

Margaret sighed. "Look, this is why I didn't want to tell you. You'd try to tell me I needed to undergo chemo or whatever treatment plan my doctor could scheme up. I saw what chemo did to Gilda and Bev, and they got lucky. They caught their cancer early. I wasn't so lucky with mine."

"So, you're just going to give up?" Adrian's nostrils flared. "I didn't peg you as a quitter, Ma."

Margaret fidgeted with her nightgown. "I'm not

expecting you to understand, but I *am* asking you to respect my decision."

That was just like her. It was okay for her to have an opinion about everything Adrian ever did, or didn't do for that matter, but when the tables were turned, her choices were never up for debate.

"Fine."

"Okay, then."

"Okay." Adrian grabbed her purse. "I'm going out. Do you need anything?"

"No, I'm good."

"If you change your mind, just call me."

Margaret nodded. Adrian studied her, seeing a hint of fear behind her eyes. She realized her mother must be scared, knowing her time was running out. Without thinking, Adrian wrapped her arms around her mother, partly to comfort herself but mostly to comfort her mother. Stunned, it took Margaret a few moments to lift one hand and place it on her daughter's shoulder. Adrian pulled back, looked her mother in the eyes and forced a smile. She squeezed her shoulder and left.

Once out of sight, Adrian felt a tear stream down her face. The toughness instilled in her by her mother still ran deep. She still couldn't cry in front of her, even after hearing she wouldn't fight the cancer. With her health rapidly deteriorating, Margaret needed to lean on a pillar of strength, not a puddle of tears. Could Adrian really handle the last stretch of her mother's journey, supporting her as she crossed over from this life to the next?

She sat in her car, her hands on the steering wheel. She felt lost as she dialed Laura's number. "You won't believe what I found out last night," Adrian said when her friend answered. "My mom isn't going to treat her cancer."

"Wow. Oh my gosh, I'm so sorry. How are you holding up?" Dylan whimpered in the background.

"Not too good." Adrian paused, lighting a cigarette. "I just don't understand why she won't at least try to fight it."

"I'm really sorry to hear that. You know it's an uphill battle trying to convince her after she's made up her mind about something. I guess all you can do is try to be supportive of her decision, as much as you don't agree with it."

"Yeah, you're right. I just don't know how I'm supposed to help her."

There was a pause on the line. "You know, I heard something about golden milk being good for cancer."

"Golden what?" What kind of hippie remedy was Laura recommending now?

"Golden milk. It's made with turmeric, which is good for inflammation and pain management. I'll send you the recipe."

"Do I need to go to a witch doctor to get the ingredients for this or wait for a full moon or Chuck Norris's tears or something?"

"Ha-ha. Very funny. You can get everything at a grocery store." Dylan's whimpering turned into screaming. "I better go but try making the milk. I think it could at least help her feel a little better."

Adrian agreed, and they hung up.

11

A fter a successful afternoon painting at the beach, Adrian stalked the aisles at Brennan's Grocery to find the items on the list Laura sent over. Adrian felt proud of her work that afternoon and looked forward to sharing it at the next group meeting. Referring to her text, she checked coconut milk off the list and proceeded to the spice aisle to pick up other ingredients.

The concoction didn't seem too hippie-dippy. And if it helped her mother feel better, that was all that mattered. Although, getting her to drink it might present another set of challenges, but Adrian would cross that bridge later.

She rounded the corner and searched the spices for turmeric, ginger, black pepper and cinnamon. She grabbed the jars and put them in her basket, referring to the list to see what was left.

"You didn't strike me as the golden milk type." She turned to see Christian smiling at her, his cobalt blue tie slightly undone. His gray pinstripe suit jacket was unbuttoned, revealing a crisp white shirt that hugged his chiseled body in all the right places. His eyes met hers, and her skin prickled with excitement.

"I'm full of surprises." She smiled back.

"I have no doubt." He winked.

Blood rushed to her cheeks, and her stomach fluttered under his scrutiny. She noticed he had a six-pack of beer under one arm and a frozen pizza under the other. "Your evening plans look a lot more exciting than mine."

He shrugged. "What can I say? I lead a very exciting life."

Adrian laughed. He licked his lips, drawing attention to the soft fullness of his smile. She thought about those lips gently brushing against her skin and felt certain parts of her body spring to life.

Another patron excused himself past them, breaking the spell. Christian studied the contents in her basket. "You're missing coconut oil and honey. Do you already have that at home?"

She thought about her mother's coconut oil and was certain that wouldn't be Dr. Laura approved. Christian tried to decipher her micro expressions before she shook her head. "I better get them, just in case."

"Coconut oil is over there." He nodded toward the end of the aisle. "Here, mind if I...?" He motioned to her basket, asking if he could handle it for her. She nodded, and he put his items in the basket and guided her toward the oil, gently placing his hand on her back. Waves of excitement flowed through her body. She watched him bend over to grab the coconut oil and admired the view. "Honey is in aisle two," he said, leading the way again with his hand.

"It sure is nice of you to accompany me through the store."

"Don't let this place fool you," he said, looking side to side. "It can be rough."

"Yes, I've heard about geriatric gangs on the loose."

"Hey, getting poked with a cane is no joke, and I'd hate to leave a lady in danger."

"Are you speaking from personal experience?" She raised an eyebrow, still very conscious of his hand on her body.

"Maybe, but don't tell anyone. I've got a rep to protect."

She laughed as they rounded the corner toward the honey.

"You'll want local honey instead of regular." He handed her a jar. His fingers lightly brushed hers, lingering longer than necessary.

"You sound like my friend Laura."

"Laura's a smart girl, then."

She examined the contents of the basket. "I think that's it for me. What can I help you find?"

"I've got everything I need."

Her skin felt hot from his gaze. Was he also blushing, or was that her imagination?

They headed toward the checkout and waited in line. Christian told her to go ahead of him.

"So, what do you do to have to suit up every day?"

"I'm a lawyer. I took over for my uncle when he died, and I have a partner...in practice. Not that kind of partner." He cleared his throat.

"Gotcha." She smiled at his display of nerves.

"What about you?"

"I'm just taking care of my mom right now. I was living in Austin for a while, working in tech."

"I've never been to Austin, but this must be a big change of pace."

She nodded as he reached past her to grab the divider. Her knees threatened to buckle as she smelled a hint of his cologne.

The cashier gave her the total as she smacked gum. Adrian handed her a card and she swiped, staring at Christian. The cashier checked to make sure there were no bumps on the top of her blond ponytail.

Adrian looked at Christian, who seemed oblivious to the cashier's interest. He clearly had no idea how attractive he was, which only made him hotter. Adrian never liked men who knew they were good looking. His lack of awareness of his effect on women was endearing.

She waited for him to complete his transaction, and they walked out together. "It was so nice running into you again," she said.

"You can run into me anytime," he blurted. They both blushed.

She could feel the heat radiating between them, and she sensed he might ask her out. She thought about Brad, which killed the buzz in the air. "Enjoy the beer."

"Oh, I will," he said with a hint of disappointment.

She felt his eyes on her while she walked toward the car. She looked over her shoulder to see if he was still watching. He was. The chemistry between them was palpable, but she didn't have any business getting involved with anyone. She fought the urge to turn around as she got in her car and drove away.

———

Margaret shuffled into the kitchen and saw Adrian standing over a pot, watching it boil. The spices in the air tickled her nose. What kind of weird soup was she making for dinner?

"What is that smell?" she asked.

"Golden milk."

"What's golden milk?"

"Laura recommended it." Adrian stirred the pot. "She said it will help you feel better."

"I didn't ask for...whatever that is." Margaret sat down in her designated spot at the kitchen table.

"Just humor me, Ma. And if not me, do it for Laura."

Margaret scoffed as she rubbed her eyes. "Laura...since when did she become so granola?"

She thought she saw Adrian crack a smile as she ladled some milk into a mug and set it in front of her, joining Margaret at the table.

Margaret eyed the mug. "This looks like puke."

"It's not puke."

"Well, you could have fooled me." Margaret sniffed the mug. "It smells funny."

"Just drink it, will you? Look, I'll have some with you." Adrian ladled the golden concoction into a mug for herself and returned to the table. "See? We'll do it together." She held up her mug, waiting for Margaret to do the same.

"Okay, kid. It's your funeral," Margaret said, picking up her mug with a shaky hand. "Bottom's up." She clinked her mug against Adrian's and they both held eye contact while they brought their mugs to their respective lips. Margaret secretly waited for Adrian to take a sip first, just in case she keeled over at the table.

"See? This is good," Adrian said.

Margaret took a sip, feeling the warmth coat her throat. "That *is* kind of nice, I suppose." She examined her mug again. Who would have thought something so unappealing to the eye would taste so good? "What's this do again?"

"Laura said it helps with pain and some other stuff. I don't remember."

They sipped in silence. Margaret had so much she wanted to say but no clue how to say it. How could she make up for years of misunderstandings before it was too late?

"How is Laura doing, anyway?" Better to stick with safe topics for the time being.

"She's good. Dylan is growing so quickly, and somehow, she balances being a super mom with selling houses and teaching yoga."

Margaret, unsure of what to say, took another sip from her mug. She never considered herself a super mom, and in fact, there was so much she would go back and change if she could do it all over again. Why did women hold themselves to those insane standards? Margaret never participated in the stupid games women play with one another, like *How to Outdo Every Woman You Know*, or *I'm a Better Mom Than You*. She knew better than to think Laura was handling all three of those responsibilities well and being a super wife on top of that. Chances were, Laura was barely holding it together. Margaret knew that feeling all too well.

"Ma?"

Margaret shook her head. "Sorry, what were you saying?"

"I said it was really nice meeting your friends last night. When are they coming over again?"

"Oh, probably next week. They really enjoyed meeting you too, by the way."

They both went quiet again. Margaret enjoyed the warmth of the milk as it radiated through her body. She felt it gurgle in her stomach from nerves, knowing there would never be a good time to re-open old wounds. But they needed to in order for them both to heal.

"I know we haven't always seen eye to eye, and I know I have a funny way of showing it, but I hope you know I'm glad you're here." Margaret reached her hand across the table.

Adrian, dumbfounded, looked down at her mother's hand resting on hers. "I—," Her phone rang. "It's Laura."

"Go on, take it," Margaret said, retreating her hand.

Apparently, it wasn't the time. "Tell her I said thank you...for the milk."

Adrian nodded as she answered, leaving the table to head outside to smoke a cigarette, no doubt.

Margaret finished her mug, rinsing it in the sink before placing it in the dishwasher. She settled into her familiar recliner in the living room but not before pressing her ear to the front door to listen to the low hum of her daughter talking to her best friend, smiling as she heard her laugh.

————

"WELL, DID SHE LIKE IT?" Laura asked.

"Yes, we were just talking about you while we were drinking it." Adrian sensed her mother was about to say something big, reopening old wounds she wasn't sure she was ready to face. Her emotions were mixed when she answered the phone.

"Do you want to call me back?"

A part of Adrian felt relieved to be saved by the bell, so to speak. But the other part of her knew something big was about to be said. She knew there would come a time when they would need to face the past, but the thought of it terrified her. They had come to some sense of normalcy, and for them, that was saying something. She didn't want to rock the boat but knew it would have to be rocked eventually.

"Hello?"

"No, it's totally fine." Adrian grabbed the pack of cigarettes stashed in her car and lit one.

"So, she liked the milk?"

"Yeah, she said it looked like puke."

"Did you strain it?"

"Was I supposed to?"

Laura scoffed. "No wonder. Yeah, you're supposed to strain the spices out of it. Otherwise, it can be a little—"

"Chunky?"

They both laughed.

"I miss you," Laura said. "What else is going on?"

"I miss you too. And let me think...oh, you won't believe who I ran into."

"Who?"

"Christian Stephens."

"Oh, wow. Where'd you run into him?"

"At Brennan's while I was getting ingredients for the milk." Adrian didn't want to mention group therapy. She wanted to keep her conversation light despite the heaviness in her life lately.

"So? How's he look? What's he doing?"

"He's definitely not a geek anymore." Adrian blushed as she thought about him in the grey suit.

"Oh, *really*?" Laura sounded way too enthusiastic.

"Yeah, and he's a lawyer, although I don't know what kind."

"Christian Stephens is a hot lawyer...never would have guessed. So, did he ask you out?"

"What? No." Adrian would have been lying to herself if she said the thought hadn't crossed her mind, especially the way he'd looked at her when they were in the parking lot. "I'm a grieving widow. What would people think?"

"Who cares what people think? Besides, at some point you need to get your groove back."

"I won't be grooving anytime soon."

They both laughed.

"But you know who might? My mother."

"Excuse me?"

"Yep. My mother is sweet on her pot dealer."

Laura sounded like she choked. "Come again?"

"You heard me right. My mother is a pothead. And she has pothead friends. And a crush on her dealer."

"Did you skip Florida and move to Compton?"

Adrian laughed. "Apparently, a lot has changed since I've been away."

"No kidding." A timer went off in the background. "Okay, I need to go take dinner out of the oven."

"Okay, love you."

"Love you more."

12

Adrian rolled the painting she'd made for Gina for easy transport as she made her way over to the pavilion for another group therapy session. She'd felt so moved hearing Gina's story and could only imagine the pain the woman felt losing her Trudy. Adrian had shed so many tears in the past over what could have been every time she got her period, and she wasn't sure she was strong enough to endure losing a child. She hoped her painting of Trudy in a better place would help Gina find peace.

She approached the group. Henry and Susan were in deep conversation. Adrian caught bits of chatter about their support of the same candidate in the upcoming election. Karen and Frank were talking about the latest episode of some reality TV show Adrian hadn't heard of. Gina sat alone, staring off toward the shoreline in the distance. Adrian approached, placing a hand on her shoulder.

"Gina, I have to tell you—your story about Trudy really touched my heart last week."

"Thanks. She was a very special girl." Gina placed her hand on top of Adrian's.

"I made something for you."

Gina turned toward Adrian with a puzzled look as Adrian unrolled the watercolor painting of Trudy playing in a field of daffodils with the little girl Adrian had met in Heaven. "But—wow, this...it looks just like her." Gina's jaw slacked in awe, seeing her little girl happy on the other side. Tears ran down her face, pooling in her wide smile. "How did you know?"

"You painted a clear picture for me, so I thought I'd do the same for you."

"I—I don't know what to say." Gina looked back at the painting, running her fingers over her little girl. "Thank you." She reached her arm up to embrace Adrian in a hug. Adrian felt something release in Gina, a heavy weight lifting off her shoulders. She squeezed Gina tighter.

"You're welcome," she said, pulling back from Gina as they looked at the painting together again.

"You painted that?" Christian asked. His cologne tickled Adrian's senses as she felt him standing behind her. His proximity made her skin prickle with excitement as she nodded. "Wow, that's...amazing."

"Thanks," Adrian said. She blushed as they locked eyes.

"Okay, I think it's about time we get started," Karen said. Everyone took their seats, Christian sitting next to Adrian. "Today, I thought we'd spend some time talking about anniversaries and how we memorialize our loved ones. It can be tough the first time you experience an anniversary or a birthday without your loved one present, and just because they're gone doesn't mean you can't continue to celebrate. Does anyone have a way they continue to celebrate milestones for their loved one in their absence?"

Henry cleared his throat. "It was my and Betty's fortieth wedding anniversary on Monday." He fidgeted with his wedding band. "We spent our thirty-ninth in the hospital after the chemo stopped working. I always brought her a dozen roses and took her dancing after a candlelit dinner at Rock Island Grill, and our last anniversary was no different.

"I had to do some begging, but the hospital staff helped me recreate our anniversary tradition, allowing me to bring in dinner from the restaurant along with the red roses as usual. One of the nurses brought in a CD player, and I put on some of our Motown favorites. I had to give up the candles, but the look on Betty's face was enough to light up the whole hospital." He smiled before continuing. "After we ate dinner, I carefully helped my wife up from bed and we danced together, cheek to cheek, just like old times. When a nurse came into the room to let me know visiting hours were done, I mouthed 'five more minutes.' She nodded, and I held my wife closer, wishing those last five minutes would never end." He closed his eyes, holding his hand over his heart, reliving the moment in his third eye.

"That's beautiful," Frank said.

"This year, I continued the tradition," Henry said. "I brought roses to her gravesite and played the same Motown CD as I ate my usual from the Grill while I talked to her. I could almost feel her cheek pressed to mine, her delicate hands wrapped around me. God, I miss her so much."

Karen handed Henry a tissue box, and he took one, dabbing at the corners of his brown eyes.

"Better hand me one too," Gina said. "I'm sure no one's surprised I'm crying again." She giggled.

"That's so beautiful, Henry. Thank you for sharing," Karen said.

Adrian could see Henry and Betty dancing vividly in her mind's eye. He spun Betty around in a perfect circle before bringing her close again, their cocoa-skinned figures merging into one form. She knew what she needed to do.

"Well, some of you probably remember this, but it would have been my son's twenty-sixth birthday on Saturday," Karen said. "He was a total adrenaline junkie, and he always pushed the limits, nearly giving me a heart attack in the process." She chuckled. "But to honor him, I'm going skydiving this Saturday, and I'm scared to death."

The group certainly reacted at Karen's news. Frank reached over to check her pulse, and Gina and Susan said they would never consider doing something so dangerous, which was the only thing they'd ever agreed on.

"That's awesome," Christian said. "I bet Isaac would be proud."

"I think he would be too," Karen said. "And I'm forcing Lyle to go with me so one, I don't chicken out, and two, if the parachute fails, we'll go out of this world together."

Christian laughed. "The parachute won't fail. I've heard it's a life-changing experience."

"It is," Adrian said.

"You've been?" He looked over at her in surprise.

She nodded. "Laura and I went after college graduation. It was...peaceful."

"Peaceful?" Susan and Gina said in unison.

"It's hard to explain, but...yeah. Everything moves in slow motion despite how quickly you're falling. You're going to love it."

"You're full of surprises," Christian said. They locked eyes. She wasn't the only one.

"I hope you're right," Karen said. "Hopefully, you'll see me next week. If not, it's been nice knowing you all." She chuckled.

"You'll be here, probably still in one piece," Frank said.

"It's amazing what we do for our loved ones, isn't it?" Karen said.

"No doubt," Christian said, stealing a glance at Adrian. Her cheeks warmed.

After they wrapped up for the week, Adrian and Christian stayed behind to help Karen clean up.

"Who knew you were so gutsy?" he said.

"Oh, trust me, I was scared to death. It was Laura's idea." She leaned a folding chair against a pillar.

"The real question is, would you go again?" Karen asked.

"In a heartbeat."

"Wow," Christian said. "I'm impressed."

"Me too," Karen said. "Christian, would you...?"

"Got it," he said, lifting the stack of folding chairs. Adrian admired his muscles flexing through his crisp white shirt as he carried them toward Karen's car, following behind with a folding table. Karen opened the hatchback of her small SUV and he loaded the chairs. Adrian handed him the table and their fingers lightly grazed during the handoff.

"Well, that's it for me," Karen said, lowering the hatch. "I hope to see you both next week."

"You will," Adrian said before Karen took off.

And then there were two.

"That painting you did for Gina was beautiful. Where'd you learn to do that?"

"My dad was a painter. I guess it's in the genes." She shrugged. "I thought it might help her a little."

"You never cease to amaze me."

"What?" She blushed.

"I never would have pegged you as a skydiving painter."

"Well, I don't typically do those two things together."

He laughed. "I guess that wouldn't work out too well."

"I don't know, maybe that's how some of those splatter paintings are made." She shrugged and they both laughed. His gaze intensified, and Adrian's knees felt weak.

Christian's phone buzzed. "I gotta go meet a client. Stay

safe. I want to see you again." He blushed, both of them surprised at his honesty.

She nodded. "Me too." This time, she watched him walk away.

———

ADRIAN HAD a smile on her face the entire drive home. She couldn't stop thinking about Christian and how good it felt to just flirt. It felt really good to be desired again, even though it probably wouldn't go anywhere. It had been a while since she felt sexy, and when he looked at her, she felt like a goddess.

Her mood changed when she turned onto her mother's street. She saw an unfamiliar sedan with Texas plates parked along the curb outside the house. Laura drove an SUV, so it couldn't be her, could it? Maybe she'd decided to rent a car to avoid putting miles on hers. Was this all part of a surprise?

Adrian parked her car and headed toward the front door, smiling at the idea of seeing her best friend. The last few weeks had been challenging and seeing her would certainly lift her spirits. They'd have to get chili fries at The Pelican, stat.

As Adrian turned the doorknob, her smile slowly faded. Her mother sat in her usual chair, but a blond woman was on the sofa. It took Adrian a moment to recognize Celeste, one of Brad's former co-workers. She looked different than the last time Adrian saw her, which was at a Christmas party she and Brad held at their house about a year ago. Celeste's straight blond hair kissed her shoulders, and her skin looked radiant, practically glowing. What was she doing there?

"Adrian, have you met Celeste?" Margaret asked. Adrian's pulse raced. Based on her tone, she knew Margaret already knew the answer.

"Celeste...what are you doing here?"

"I'm sorry I just showed up this way, but I was afraid you wouldn't believe me if I called," Celeste said.

"She was just telling me how she knew Brad...intimately," Margaret said before Celeste.

Adrian's brow wrinkled. Clearly, she was missing something.

Celeste struggled to get up from the couch. As she stood, a very pregnant belly protruded from her small frame. Cylinders in Adrian's mind clicked: Celeste was Brad's mistress. Was she carrying his baby?

"I don't understand," Adrian said. She didn't want to believe the blatantly obvious. Maybe there was some other explanation, and she hoped the pregnant stick figure would say otherwise.

"I know this may come as a shock to you, but Brad and I were having an affair for the last year. This is his baby." Celeste rubbed her belly, obviously proud of her and Brad's creation.

Adrian waited for a punchline, but it wasn't a joke. She looked at Margaret, who avoided eye contact with either one of them. The proverbial cat was out of the bag. There was no way Adrian could continue the charade of Brad being a loving, faithful husband.

"So, why are you here? Brad's dead." Adrian felt sick, adrenaline coursing through her veins.

"Well, according to my lawyer—"

"Excuse me?"

"I have rights. Well, my child has rights." Celeste placed a hand on her side as she winced from discomfort.

"But he's dead. What do you want from me?"

"I'm due financial support. From his estate, perhaps."

Celeste had to know Brad wasn't worth much. That had to have come up at some point during their pillow talk. Adrian couldn't help feeling like this was personal somehow. Celeste had a good job from what she could recall. Why would she do this?

"I know this is a lot to process. Maybe we should sit down and talk about it." Her saccharine tone made Adrian want to vomit.

"You can't be serious?" Adrian couldn't hold back anymore. Seeing the reality of her late husband's infidelity staring her in the face reopened wounds that had barely scabbed over. Pain oozed from them, threatening to drain her dry.

Adrian looked at Margaret, who sat quietly in her chair, concentrating on one spot on the floor.

"I assure you, I'm very serious." Celeste stepped forward. "I thought maybe we could discuss this without lawyers getting involved, but I guess that's not a possibility."

"Don't you dare make this about me. You're the one who fucked my husband and got yourself into this mess. You really thought I'd just accept you—it—with open arms?"

Celeste paused. "I thought maybe—"

"How the hell do I know that's really his child you're carrying anyway?"

"Brad was the only man I've been with in the last year."

"Whatever." Adrian crossed her arms. "I want proof. I want to see a paternity test."

"But I just told you—"

"I don't care!" Adrian couldn't take it anymore. "You know what? Get out." She grabbed Celeste by the arm, pulling her toward the door.

"Adrian!" Margaret yelled.

"Let go of me! Ow!" Celeste tried to pull away. Adrian dragged her toward the front door and pushed her out.

"You'll definitely be hearing from my lawyer." Celeste smoothed her hair.

"Can't wait!" Adrian slammed the door in her face. Adrian took deep breaths as she tried to push the rage monster back. Guilt from her outburst set in, and tears welled in her eyes. She didn't know how to process the multitude of emotions coursing through her body. Brad and Celeste. Really?

It had been easier when she didn't know who it was. But, of course, Brad's affair was a total cliché of someone he worked with. How had that even started? Who came onto who first? She shook her head, avoiding her imagination as it threatened to run away.

To make matters worse, he got Celeste pregnant with ease. She now carried everything Adrian always wanted with Brad. Adrian was the problem all along. It had nothing to do with him. She felt sick.

She looked at Margaret, who had a disgusted look on her face. She braced herself for the impending storm ahead.

13

"I know you want to say something, so just say it."

Margaret shook her head. "You know, I hate to say I told you so, but..." she shrugged.

"Oh my God. Are you serious?"

"Well, I knew Brad was no good for you, and there went proof."

"You are choosing this moment, after what just happened, to gloat?"

"I'm not gloating." Margaret paused. She let out a breath and shook her head. "You obviously knew Brad cheated, though, didn't you?"

Adrian sputtered something incomprehensible, feeling exposed.

"You know how I know? Because you didn't seem that surprised by his affair, only by the baby."

"What do you want me to say, Ma? You're right? Okay, fine, you're right. You're right about everything. Are you happy now?"

"No. Why would that make me happy?" Margaret's tone was much more controlled than her daughter's.

"I don't understand you," Adrian spat. "What do you want from me?"

"How about honesty?"

"Oh, you want to talk about honesty? What about your lack of treatment? If it weren't for Gilda, I still wouldn't even know about that, would I?"

Margaret paused. "That has nothing to do with this." She looked away.

"Doesn't it, though? We're talking about honesty, right? Or does honesty only apply to me and not to you?"

"Okay, then. Since we're getting things out in the open, do you want to know why I didn't tell you about your father's illness? Because he asked me not to."

Adrian's stomach plummeted. "What do you mean?"

"His doctor found an arrhythmia, and he didn't want to worry you. He'd been taking some medication to help with it for a few months, and we'd been working on lifestyle adjustments, but his heart just gave out. His doctor did everything he could to save him, but it obviously wasn't enough."

Adrian's jaw dropped. Her father didn't want to worry her with his health? What was more important than that? She sat on the edge of the sofa, in shock, as the memory replayed in her mind. She thought about her father's funeral and how ugly she was to her mother. She'd blamed Margaret for robbing her of the opportunity to say goodbye. She even cut her mother out of her life because of that lie. Adrian felt ashamed at her behavior in retrospect. "Why didn't you tell me?"

"Like you would have listened? I'd grown quite accustomed to being the bad guy over the years, anyway. It was always you two against me." Margaret's eyes watered.

"That's so typical of you. You should have tried harder to tell me. You should have called. Hell, you could have sent me a letter, an email, anything. But you didn't, and now you expect me to feel sorry for you?"

"Don't you dare talk to me that way," Margaret said and coughed. Her eyes grew wide as she tried to catch her breath.

Seeing her struggle diffused Adrian's anger, and she felt guilty at her outburst. She grabbed the glass of water next to her mother's chair and handed it to her, rubbing her back until the coughing stopped. Margaret took a sip once she caught her breath, and then she cleared her throat.

"I'm sorry, Ma. Are you okay?"

"I'm dying, Adrian." Margaret looked into her eyes with a weak smile. "How's that for honesty?"

Tears welled in Adrian's eyes, the reality of her mother's condition setting in. "What can I do?"

"Call a lawyer, and make sure that child is really his."

Adrian hugged her mother, and it was the first time in her entire life that she let go of Margaret first.

———

ADRIAN FIXED a simple dinner while Margaret rested in her chair. The events of the afternoon had taken a toll on both of them in different ways. Adrian still couldn't believe Brad had been unfaithful with Celeste. She'd thought she knew her husband better than that. But then again, how well can you really know anyone?

She thought about all the times Brad worked late. He and Celeste were on the same team, and come to think of it, he would casually mention her more than the rest of his co-workers. Celeste probably pulled some Sharon Stone leg crossing move on Brad, leaving him speechless. Adrian shuddered at the thought, wanting to slap her dead husband for his stupidity.

But then again, wasn't she being a little unfair? How did she know it wasn't him who initiated what happened? Adrian knew better than anyone how charismatic Brad could be. She fell hard and fast for him long ago. He was determined, never settling for anything less than what he wanted. Once he'd decided what he wanted, of course. So, he probably set his sights on Celeste, and the rest was history.

Regardless of the details, it didn't change the fact that Celeste gotten pregnant and obviously wanted some kind of financial support. How could they even prove paternity with him six feet under? Would they have to exhume his body? That would go over like a lead balloon with his parents. *Your philandering son got his slutty co-worker pregnant, so we need to dig up his bones to prove paternity.* Adrian cracked a smile thinking of his mother's reaction. She'd love to hear his mother explain that to her girlfriends at the club.

And then there was Adrian's father. She still felt her mother could have tried harder to tell her about George's illness, but she saw her point. Why did her father insist on not telling her? Maybe she could have done something for him sooner, and he'd still be there. He always put himself last, giving every ounce of himself to Margaret and Adrian. In the end, he gave a little more of himself to Margaret, and she honored her husband's wishes, knowing how it could potentially ruin the already strained relationship she had with Adrian.

Adrian marveled at the sacrifice Margaret made in the name of love for her husband. God had other plans for her father, and even though his death initially pushed them apart, they were together now for a reason. Would she allow their stubbornness to push them apart again? Her mother had always been a bit of a mystery to her, and if she'd learned anything since she'd arrived, there was so much more about Margaret she wanted to understand before it was too late. Chances were, she wasn't the only one feeling that way. She knew she had to do her part to be vulnerable. She could only hope that Margaret would follow her lead.

"Ma, dinner is ready." Adrian plated spaghetti as Margaret shuffled into the kitchen and sat in her usual chair. Adrian set the plates down and joined in her usual seat to the left. They twirled noodles around forks in silence. The sun began its descent, and the streetlights sparked with life.

Adrian set her fork down. "I'm sorry."

"For what?" Margaret mumbled through a mouthful of spaghetti.

"For not making it easier to tell me about Dad. I know I wouldn't have listened in that moment. You were right about that."

Margaret took a sip from her water glass. "Yeah, I'm sorry too. I could have tried harder to tell you. I just didn't think you'd listen."

"You weren't wrong about that, but I wish you would have said something, even after the fact."

"Would you have listened?"

"Of course, I would have. I always listen to you, don't I?" Adrian cracked a smile.

Margaret's shoulders relaxed, her lips curling into a smile. "I'll remember that."

Adrian picked up her fork. "I'm glad we're talking now, though."

Margaret placed a bony hand on top of Adrian's, waiting for their eyes to meet. "Me too."

They both smiled, feeling their relationship begin to thaw.

Adrian cleared the table after dinner and started the dishwasher before stepping outside to call Laura. She grabbed her pack of cigarettes from the car, lighting one as she dialed the phone. "You won't believe the day I've had," she said when Laura answered. She sat down by the front door, exhaling billows of smoke. "Celeste, one of Brad's old co-workers, showed up here, pregnant, saying the baby is Brad's."

"Wait, what now?"

"You heard correctly, my friend."

"Well, at least you know who the mystery woman is now."

"Yeah, how cliché of Brad to have an affair with his co-worker." Adrian watched a puff of smoke head out over the sidewalk.

"And she's pregnant?"

"Yep, looked to be about six months along."

"The plot thickens."

"You have no idea." Adrian rubbed her temple.

"Well, if we're doing simple math, chances are Celeste told Brad, so he probably knew about the baby before he died."

Adrian's heart sank. "I hadn't even thought about that." So even Brad knew Celeste gave him something Adrian had been unable to. No, thank God she hadn't. She couldn't imagine trying to raise his spawn after finding out all of this about him.

"But this is assuming she's not lying. If I were you, I'd get a lawyer. Speaking of...didn't you tell me Christian was a lawyer?"

"Yeah, he is, although I don't know what kind." Christian. Maybe he would be able to help her make sense of this.

"I've been thinking you should call him anyway, but now you have a legitimate legal reason to seek his counsel."

"I can practically hear your eyebrows wiggling over here." They both laughed.

"But seriously, you can't do this on your own. You need to have someone in your corner who's got your back. Don't just take her word for it. People lie."

"You're right about that." Adrian put out her cigarette. "I'll call him."

"At least he'll be nice to look at while he's fighting for your honor."

"No doubt." Adrian thought about Christian in his pinstripe suits. "Thank you for your sage wisdom."

"That's what I'm here for, girl. Now, go get 'em."

"Peace begins with me, right?"

Laura echoed the mantra before they hung up. Adrian knew it was no accident she ran into Christian a couple of weeks ago. Hopefully, he could help her out of this mess.

14

The following week, Adrian sat in the quaint waiting room of Kellogg, Stephens and Associates, waiting for her name to be called. There weren't too many frills in the waiting area. It had stark white walls and brown faux leather chairs with just enough cushion to make the wait more bearable. The office was located in an old bungalow style house, with a large bay window overlooking the coastal drag. Fortunately, Christian had a cancellation, and his assistant was able to fit her in on short notice.

She tried to distract her mind with two-month old copies of *US Weekly* to no avail. She set them down in defeat. Not even Hollywood drama held a candle to her own. What if the baby was really Brad's? Would she be forced to be some sort of twisted proxy, supporting it for the rest of her life?

She'd grown accustomed to not wearing power suits and attending meetings to discuss other pointless meetings. She liked where life had taken her, allowing her to explore the idea of trading in her briefcase for a paint brush. The life she'd always envisioned for herself was within reach, and a love child's tiny hand could snatch it all away from her in an instant.

Contrary to recent events, she'd always been a relatively lucky person. Things always lined up for her, even in the bleakest of moments. She always persevered, finding a way to come out of a pile of garbage smelling like roses. She wasn't about to let her luck run out. There had to be a way out of the current mess.

"Adrian, Christian will see you now." His assistant interrupted her train of thoughts. Adrian followed her, a lanky older woman with chestnut hair pulled back in a tight bun wearing entirely too much makeup, as she took her back to his office. Christian motioned for Adrian to come in despite cradling a phone receiver between his shoulder and right ear. She felt his eyes trail over her entire body as she sat in front of his desk. She smiled at him, and he made a rolling gesture with his hand to indicate he was wrapping up the call. She mouthed "take your time," and his eyes lingered on her lips. He was only charging her by the hour, right?

She looked around his office while she waited. It wasn't a typical lawyer's office. It didn't have an ounce of stuffiness to it, despite the obvious age of the building. It was surprisingly bright and airy, with cream colored walls and blue accents reminiscent of a coastal escape. He didn't have any personal photographs anywhere, although a lone nail hammered into the wall left a reminder of what used to be. His diplomas were prominently displayed, including a law degree from Stetson University, and white bookcases lined one of the walls with prolific volumes on law. Oddly enough, a copy of *Oh, The Places You'll Go!* by Dr. Seuss stood prominently on one of the shelves. Adrian giggled, looking back at Christian, who hadn't taken his eyes off her the whole time.

He finally hung up. "Sorry about that."

"You didn't strike me as a Dr. Seuss kind of guy."

He gave her a confused look, and she pointed to the book on the middle shelf on his bookcase.

"Oh, that." He chuckled. "My aunt Beverly gave that to me when I graduated from Law School.

"It's a classic."

He shifted in his seat, clearly entering into lawyer mode. "I want to start off by saying today's consult will be at no charge." He held up a hand to cut off her protests. "I insist, and it's not up for debate or discussion. With that said, this isn't my normal area of expertise, but I'm happy to help as much as I can."

"Thank you. I truly appreciate it."

"My pleasure. So, tell me about this pregnant mistress."

She recounted her interaction with Celeste, and he took diligent notes while she spoke. She felt vulnerable when she told him how Brad had confessed his infidelity moments before their crash. She hadn't planned on telling anyone other than Laura about that, but something about Christian made her feel completely at ease. She could talk to him about anything, and she sensed there was no judgment.

His eyes met hers, expressing deep empathy for being cheated on. "Did Brad have a will, by chance?" Adrian shook her head, and he scribbled some notes. "And what assets did he have?"

"He had a car that was paid off, and we had a joint bank account and owned a house together."

"No 401k or anything like that?"

"No, we had a combined Roth IRA account we both contributed to on a monthly basis."

"And what about the house? Did you own that free and clear?"

She shifted in her seat. "Sorta. We opted for the mortgage insurance that pays the balance in the event that one of us died."

He scribbled more notes. "And have you sold the house, or do you still own it?"

"I have it currently listed on the market, but it hasn't sold yet."

"Did you have health insurance?"

"Yes, and I had about $50,000 in medical expenses beyond what was covered by our policies."

"Gotcha." He cradled his face in his hand and furrowed his brow. He was kinda sexy when he was deep in thought. "So, this is not a typical paternity and child support case, since the father is deceased." He looked over his notes again. "I know how things would be handled here in Florida, but since this happened in Texas, it would be in accordance with Texas law."

"That makes sense."

"But typically, the child would be due a percentage of net income on a monthly basis from the father, but since he's deceased, Celeste could come after a portion of his assets. Have you gone through probate yet?"

"I didn't see the need, since all of our assets were in both of our names."

He made another note. "And did Brad have a life insurance policy?"

"Yes, but the majority of the funds were used on our medical expenses from the accident."

"Hmm...okay. So, the biggest assets are your house and IRA. But first things first—we need to prove paternity, and we can't do that without a body or a baby."

"So, what can I do?"

"I'd advise you to wait it out for now. We can't do anything until the baby is born anyway." He leaned back slightly in his chair.

Waiting had never been her forte, and she felt herself deflate. "Celeste was pretty certain he was the father, and I'm sure she would know."

"Don't be so sure. Have you ever seen daytime talk shows?"

Adrian laughed, and it was the hardest she'd laughed in a couple of weeks. "Point taken. You didn't strike me as a daytime TV kind of guy."

"What can I say? I'm full of surprises." He smiled and reached his hand across the desk and covered hers. Heat radiated through her body from his touch, making her knees weak. "Don't worry. We will figure this out together."

They locked eyes, and in that moment, she no longer felt alone.

———

ADRIAN LADLED golden milk into two mugs, placing one in front of her mother before joining her at the dining table.

"More golden milk, I see." Margaret wrinkled her nose. "Why are we drinking this again?" Her voice sounded a little wheezy.

"Because Laura said it's good for our immune systems." They'd established a ritual of drinking the milk after dinner. Neither one of them expected it to be a cure-all by any means, but if it bought them a little more time together it was worth it. The fact that they wanted to spend more time together, and Adrian noticed Margaret had been sleeping better, made her chalk it up as a win.

"How did your meeting go with Christian today?"

"It went well, or as well as it could have, anyway. He told me basically to just sit and wait. Celeste hasn't officially filed anything yet, so there's really nothing for me to do."

Margaret snickered. "Yeah, like you're so good at waiting." Adrian stuck out her tongue and they both giggled. "What about the paternity?"

"We'd have to wait for the baby to be born, and then we'd most likely have to exhume Brad's body to prove it."

"Wow, and if the baby is his after all is said and done, what then?"

"She'd be entitled to a portion of his estate, which would include our house and potentially our retirement funds since the majority of his life insurance policy paid our medical bills." Adrian rubbed the back of her neck.

"Rats." Margaret looked disappointed. "He's even worse than I thought, leaving you with this mess to clean up."

"Didn't you teach me to not speak ill of the dead?"

"Yeah, but now I've got the sick old lady card to play and can say whatever I want."

"And you're milking it, aren't you?" Adrian smirked. They finished their drinks, and Adrian placed the empty mugs in the dishwasher. "If you don't need anything else at the moment, I'm going to call Laura."

"Try to smoke only one cigarette this time. Remember, all this could be yours." Margaret waved her hands over her body like Vanna White.

Adrian rolled her eyes. "Thanks, Ma." She stepped outside and retrieved her not-so-secret stash of cigarettes. As the phone rang, she brought a cigarette to her lips and heard her mother hacking up a lung inside. The cigarette suddenly lost its appeal, and she slipped it back in the pack.

Laura answered. "So, how was it?"

"As good as I could expect at this point." She recapped the details of the meeting, including the wait and see approach.

"And how are you handling that?"

"I guess I don't have a choice, so I'll have to dig deep to find patience."

"Who knows. Maybe she's lying and it's not his baby."

"Christian said that too." She re-told his joke about daytime talk shows. "He's so funny," she mused.

"I like the sound of this."

"Yeah, he seems really smart, and I'm happy to have someone like him in my corner."

"I'm not talking about that. I'm talking about you. This is the most chipper you've sounded in a while."

"Well, I guess it's nice to feel like someone is going to fight for me and my interests."

"Are you sure it has nothing to do with the fact that he's hot?"

"I don't know what you're talking about." Adrian blushed.

"I Googled him. Nicely done. Think you can get him to hold you in contempt?"

Before Adrian could answer, a car approached her mother's house. Christian was in the driver's seat. Adrian sat up a little straighter at the sight of him, running her fingers through her hair. What was he doing there?

"Hello?"

"Sorry, I need to call you back." Adrian hung up the phone as they met each other in the driveway. "A house-call on a Wednesday evening? You sure are dedicated to your clients."

"Well, that's why I'm here, actually." Adrian's heart dropped as she watched Christian look down at the ground and shift uncomfortably. "I'm going to have to defer your case to my colleague, Brian. I think he'll be a better fit to represent you, whatever happens with it."

"Oh," she said, finding it difficult to hide her disappointment. "Can I ask why?"

"Well, I have a conflict of interest."

"What do you mean?"

"I'm not very good at this," he said, smiling nervously. "And my timing is terrible, I know. But I'm hoping that you might be interested in having dinner with me sometime." He looked down at the ground, bracing himself for bad news, which was so endearing.

"I'd love to." The words fell out of her mouth without a thought, her response surprising them both. Maybe it was a good thing she didn't have time to overthink it, knowing she'd probably talk herself out of a good time. Besides, it was just dinner, right?

"Great," he said, his confidence appearing to return. "I will transfer all your case details to Brian tomorrow morning and let him know we're just waiting things out with Celeste for the time being. And how about Saturday night?"

"Yes, that sounds good." Her pulse raced.

"Okay, I'll pick you up at 7:30."

They shared an awkward goodbye reminiscent of two teenagers parting in the hallway outside of fifth period. As she watched him drive away, she called Laura back. "You won't believe what just happened." She felt seventeen again, musing about her upcoming date with her best friend.

15

After taking care of some housekeeping for Margaret, Adrian headed toward the beach to work on her latest painting. It was mid-morning, and the sun was already blazing. Summer had arrived, even though it was only mid-March. Some people joked that Florida only had two temperatures: hot and hotter. Adrian couldn't disagree, especially on a balmy morning like this one. She took off her cover-up, determined to work on her tan while she painted.

She took a deep breath before using a pencil to sketch Henry and Betty dancing in Heaven. His story touched her heart, and she hoped the painting would touch his too. Seeing the love in his eyes as he recounted his last dance with his wife left Adrian hopeful that she could find a love like that. Whenever she was ready, of course.

Resolved with her sketch, she prepared her paints, including two jars for water. As her paintbrush drifted over the canvas, her thoughts drifted toward Christian. Part of her was so flattered by his invitation, and she was amazed there was no hesitation in her acceptance. However, she couldn't help wondering in the light of a new day if it was all happening too soon.

The dirt on Brad's grave had barely settled, and there she was, accepting a date from another man. What would people think? In other people's eyes, they were a perfect couple, and only three people knew of his infidelity. Well, four with Christian's partner taking over as her counsel.

Christian.

There certainly was something about him that made her feel completely at ease. His warm, protective presence invited her in, as if he could shield her from every care in the world. When he'd asked her out to dinner, he'd looked like an awkward teenager, which made him even more adorable in her eyes. How could a man that gorgeous be remotely unsure of himself?

Regardless of their obvious chemistry, was she truly ready to put herself out there again? She still felt pain from what Brad did, and now had a physical embodiment of his infidelity growing in someone else's belly.

Allegedly.

Right?

The timing certainly wasn't ideal. She had her mother to worry about on top of everything else. Margaret's condition certainly wasn't getting any better, and Adrian would have to face the fact that her mother would make her way to Heaven soon. Would the same little girl be there to greet her too? Maybe she should share that experience with her mother. She couldn't remember the last time Margaret had talked about spirituality and had no clue what her beliefs were on what lies beyond the veil.

She painted the figures dancing together in a golden field. Maybe it wouldn't hurt to have a little fun. The last several months had been so heavy, and she could use some levity. It was just dinner. It wasn't like they were going to get married or anything. What was the harm in sharing a meal with an old high school friend?

Although the way he made her feel was certainly more than friendly. Every brief touch set fire to her skin, leaving goosebumps in its wake. But that didn't mean they had to act on those impulses. Besides, she didn't know much about him. Maybe he had some bad habits, like leaving the toilet seat up or squeezing toothpaste from the top of the tube. Oh, who was she kidding? Like any of that mattered. He was probably perfect and never farted or burped and said lustful things like, "Don't worry, I'll take care of the dishes," and, "Here, let me pour you more wine and give you a back rub." She smiled at the thought.

There was no denying something was there, but she needed to take her time. She'd barely sewn the pieces of her heart back together and couldn't take someone ripping it apart again.

She'd just have to be honest. That wouldn't be too hard, would it?

———

ADRIAN QUIETLY CELEBRATED as she carefully placed her painting across the backseat. She admired her creation, feeling proud of her accomplishment. She imagined the look on Henry's face when she would give him the painting at the next group meeting. Her heart warmed, feeling like she was finally living her destiny. She could get used to this.

When she got home, she saw Margaret, Bev, and Gilda playing cards at the dining table. They were excitedly talking about something, completely oblivious to her presence. The smile on her mother's face was infectious. Margaret looked to be almost glowing. It was good to see her spirits up, and Adrian thanked God for her mother's friends, as rowdy as they may be.

"And just what are you girls talking about?" Adrian asked, approaching the table. They all sat up a bit straighter, as if their roles were reversed, and she was the parental figure busting them for doing some illicit activity. Knowing them, it was entirely possible.

"Nothing," Margaret responded, her eyes shifty.

"Oh, come on Margie," Gilda said. "We were talking about Harold," she said to Adrian, holding her hand over her mouth as if hiding the response from the rest of the table.

"Oh, really? What about him?" Adrian raised an eyebrow.

"Adrian has a date tomorrow night," Margaret said before anyone else could answer, throwing her daughter to the wolves.

"Oh, really?" Gilda said with a raised eyebrow, mimicking Adrian. "Sit down, sit down, and tell Gilda all about it." She motioned for Adrian to take the chair next to her. Adrian looked at Margaret with wide eyes. Her mother shrugged and gave her a smug smile. Gilda practically pulled Adrian down into the chair as Adrian's cheeks turned various shades of red. "So, who is this fella, anyway?" Gilda leaned in, her chin resting on her hand.

"Christian. He's a friend...from high school." Adrian chose her words carefully, trying to strike a balance between just enough detail to satisfy their inquisitive minds and retaining some level of privacy.

"My nephew?" Bev piped up. "Oh, he's always had a thing for you, you know." She smiled conspiratorially.

"Really?" Adrian wondered what Christian shared with Bev, and if it was anything recent.

"The plot thickens!" Gilda proclaimed, hands thrown in the air. "So, where is he taking you?"

"To dinner." Adrian tried to cut the conversation as short as possible. The three of them looked at her, waiting for more detail. They could probably wait forever, so she gave in. "He mentioned some restaurant on the beach. I don't really know much other than that."

"Well, if it's Rock Island Grill, he means business," Gilda said. "He will expect you to put out."

Adrian's stomach dropped. Was she serious? He didn't seem like the type who would expect that sort of thing from a first date. While they'd known each other for years, they didn't really *know* each other. Had expectations from first dates changed that much since she'd been out of the game? Her pulse raced. Was it hot in there?

"Christian isn't that kind of guy." Bev shook her head. "He's a gentleman."

Adrian forced a smile at her words of assurance, letting out a breath she didn't realize she'd been holding.

"He may be a gentleman, but any man knows there's no place that makes the panties drop like Rock Island Grill." Gilda's eyebrows wagged.

"Stop it. You're scaring the poor girl," Bev scolded, slapping Gilda on the wrist.

Adrian grew pale, looking at her mother for help. Margaret just shrugged. She swallowed a lump in her throat. "I know I've been out of the game a little while, but is that really expected these days?"

"Take it from me, honey. He's serious," Gilda said. Bev shook her head in disagreement, leaving Adrian conflicted.

"Let's go back to talking about Harold. That sounded much more interesting."

"How long has it been for you?" Gilda asked, ignoring Adrian's attempt to change the subject.

"How long since what?"

"Since you've had sex."

"Gilda, really," Margaret chided. Finally.

Gilda brushed her off. "I'm waiting."

"Oh, I don't know…" The last thing Adrian wanted to do was talk about her sex life in front of her mother.

"If you have to think about it, it's time to get the cobwebs out of there."

"This is the company you keep?" Adrian asked Margaret, pointing at Gilda.

Margaret grinned. "Happily."

"Coconut oil is a nice all-natural lubricant. Take it from me, kid." Gilda said.

"I can't trust coconut oil coming from any of you," Adrian said. Bev laughed heartily, and they all followed suit. "At this point I'm dipping a pinkie toe in the dating pool. I'm not ready to dive in just yet."

"I want to hear all the details. Or at least, what you feel like sharing." Bev gave Adrian a hopeful smile. "Christian is a good boy. He deserves someone nice like you."

"Thanks. We'll see what happens." Adrian shrugged. She tried to keep her excitement at bay as much as possible. But thinking about his smile, his broad shoulders and strong arms enveloping her while his eyes looked at her with adoration made diving into the deep end seem inevitable.

16

Adrian attempted to steady her hand as she applied eyeliner, but it slipped, and she resolved herself to the cat eyed look that evening. It had been a while since her last first date, and she looked in the mirror and shrugged. Not too shabby. She finally left the bathroom to get a second opinion from her mother, whose eyes were glued to the TV. She cleared her throat to get attention. "Do I look okay?"

Margaret shrugged. "Sure."

"Thanks for the vote of confidence." Maybe she should put on a different dress. Again. For the seventh time.

"Sorry. You look mahhhvelous dahhling."

"Thanks, Ma." Adrian sat on the sofa, fidgeting as she waited. "When are you expecting the girls?"

"In about a half hour or so. When are you leaving?"

"In a hurry to get rid of me or something?"

"No, just curious is all." Margaret maintained eye contact with the weatherman on TV. If Adrian didn't know any better, she'd suspect her mother seemed a bit nervous too.

"I was joking, you know."

The doorbell rang. Adrian's pulse raced as she stood.

"Take a deep breath. You'll be fine." Margaret's kind

words took Adrian by surprise. She opened the door to see Christian on the other side. She exhaled, suddenly feeling calm when their eyes locked. He looked perfect in a light blue polo shirt that was tucked into a pair of dark wash jeans. His curly hair was still a little damp, and hints of his cologne tickled her senses.

"Wow, you look..." He trailed off, his gaze traveling over her body. She blushed, feeling confident in her seventh dress change: A pale-yellow maxi dress drawing attention to her collarbone and shoulders.

"You too," she admired.

"Good evening, Mrs. Russo," Christian said to Margaret.

"And what exactly are your intentions toward my daughter?" Margaret crossed her arms, feigning sternness as Adrian rolled her eyes.

"Honorable, ma'am. Scout's honor." He held his hands up in the proper salute.

"Have her back home at a reasonable hour."

"Of course."

"Okay, that's enough. Bye, Ma." Adrian pulled the door shut behind them.

You can tell a lot about someone from their car. Christian's was a practical sedan with nice upgrades, but nothing too flashy. A modest choice for someone who could probably afford more based on his profession, and the smell of his cologne hung in the air. Everything was meticulous. Not even an old drug store receipt sat on the floorboard, and there were no old gum wrappers abandoned in the cup holders.

"So, where are you taking me this evening?"

"A place right on the beach in an old 1940s bungalow called Rock Island Grill. It came highly recommended, so I figured we'd check it out."

Adrian's eyes grew wide and her pulse raced. That was

the place Gilda mentioned. Would he really expect her to put out on the first date? She swallowed hard, forcing a smile. "Sounds great." She could barely concentrate on their conversation on the way over, her mind racing with possible and probable expectations. Their elbows grazed on the center console a couple of times and sent shivers up her arm, which did nothing for her concentration. A drink would definitely help calm her nerves.

He pulled up to the front of the restaurant, handing his keys to a valet as he walked around and opened the door for Adrian. He guided her into the restaurant by placing his hand on the small of her back. His touch felt intoxicating, and she had to concentrate to walk. He asked the hostess for a table on the patio overlooking the ocean.

The sun inched closer to the horizon as it began its daily descent. The ocean swelled against the shore, and traces of salt and oleander lingered in the air. Beach grass swayed gently on sand dunes, framing couples standing near the shoreline to catch the sunset. Christian's hands inched closer to Adrian's across their blue and gold mosaic bistro table, threatening to meet as they made small talk.

Their waiter, a stocky man with a thick mustache and a newsboy hat, interrupted with the specials for the evening. Christian took the liberty of ordering a bottle of Pinot Grigio.

"You read my mind." Adrian smiled.

"One of my many talents."

"Oh, yeah? What else are you holding out on me?"

"You'll see." He winked.

Her body fluttered with nerves as she bit her lip. Her mind raced with the infinite possibilities in that two-word sentence. Was she ready to open Pandora's Box?

Their waiter uncorked the bottle of wine at the table. Christian told him to just pour after he offered to let him taste it first, and he filled two wine glasses. He raised his glass, and she mimicked him.

"What should we drink to?"

Before he could answer, elevated voices pulled their attention to an adjacent table. A middle-aged woman with blond waves cascading down her back sat opposite a stout man, whose bald spot blinded Adrian more than the setting sun.

"Are you crazy? This is our second date!"

"But when you know, you know," he said. "And I knew the moment I saw you."

"That's just creepy." The blonde stood.

"Don't go, Cathy. I love you." The bald man reached for her. His belly bumped the table, knocking Cathy's drink onto her gossamer coral dress. Adrian spotted the glint of a diamond ring on the table as Cathy stormed off. The man sat down, head hung low, as a waiter approached the table to clean up the mess. "Bring me a double martini, two olives, please," he said, and the waiter made quick work with his order. "Didn't mean to give everyone a show tonight with dinner."

"Poor guy," Christian said.

"Bold move proposing on the second date."

"I better flag down the waiter and call off my plans." Christian's eyes grew wide as he pretended to grab the waiter's attention, mouthing "no dessert."

Adrian laughed, playfully grabbing his hands from his mock call-off. "I just don't see how anyone could want to propose after one date."

"But you heard him. When you know, you know, right?" He shrugged, a smile tugging at his lips.

"Do I need to be concerned about our second date?"

"God, no. I can be a bold man, but even *I'm* not that

bold." He laced his fingers with hers. "I'd at least wait until our third date."

"Good. I know not to take this any further than our next date, then."

"You're already telling me we'll have a second date?"

She blushed. "As long as you really called off the proposal this evening."

"Yeah, don't worry. I'll just drown my sorrows in this glass of wine. Care to join me?"

Adrian raised her glass. "What are we drinking to?"

His thumb caressed her palm. "How about to taking this one date at a time?"

"Now that's a proposal I can accept." They both laughed as their glasses clinked.

Their waiter took their dinner order, and Adrian seized the opportunity to ask Christian a question that had been on her mind since they ran into each other. "Since you know my story, I think it's only fair you tell me yours. What brought you to group?"

Christian let go of her hand, leaning back in his chair. "I suppose that's fair."

"If you don't want to—"

"No, it's okay." He took a deep breath. "I started going to group when my uncle Jim died. He was like a dad to me, since my dad and I never really got along too well. He had a heart attack, and his death hit me hard."

"Sorry to hear."

"To make matters worse, the woman I was dating at the time, Sarah, confessed to cheating on me on the same day."

"Wow, that must have been rough," she said.

Christian nodded. "I thought she was the one. I was *this close* to buying her a ring, and I'm glad I didn't. It was a lot to process all at once."

"I can only imagine." She reached her hand across the table, placing it on his.

Christian held her hand in return. "When he died, I was considering an opportunity for the District Attorney, but I couldn't let everything he built go to waste. I knew I had to take his place at the firm. It was the right thing to do, and I think he'd be proud."

"I'm sure he would be."

"The group helped me work through it, even though I'm not that vocal and don't share very often."

"Like Gina?"

He smiled. "You're too new to crack jokes." They both chuckled. "What you did for her was very sweet, by the way. Where'd you learn to paint like that?"

She shrugged. "My father was a painter, so I guess it's in my blood."

"I'd like to see some of your other work sometime."

"I'm sure that could be arranged." She smiled.

Conversation flowed easily as they finished their glasses of wine with their meals. They caught the remainder of the sunset, and the waiter returned to light a candle in the center of the table and clear their plates.

"Wow, mood lighting. You're pulling out all the stops, aren't you?"

"Special place for a special lady." He grinned. "So, I heard from my aunt about your mom. It's sweet of you to take care of her."

"Thanks. We haven't always had the best relationship, which has made it a bit challenging at times."

"You've got a shot at making peace with her. Don't take that for granted."

"Yeah, it's been tough, but every day gets a little easier. Surprisingly, we're making small strides, which makes it all worth it."

Christian picked up his wine glass. "I'd like to propose another toast. To you, Adrian. You're a remarkable woman, and I'm glad we ran into each other again."

She blushed. "Cheers." Her skin prickled with heat from his gaze.

The waiter arrived with the check, and her heart sank. Christian quickly slid a credit card into the fold. "I'm not ready for the evening to end. Are you?" he asked. Adrian shook her head. "Would you be up for a walk on the beach?"

"I'd love that." She smiled. They headed toward the beach after paying the bill, leaving their shoes on the side of the stairs by the restaurant. He grabbed her hand, their fingers lacing effortlessly, as they walked toward the shore. The night sky twinkled with magic as it enveloped the last remains of the day. Her toes sank into the sand with every step as they plodded toward the shore, her dress billowing in the gentle evening breeze. It was the perfect setup for what was likely to come next, and her heart pounded. Was she ready for it?

"Christian, let's stop for a moment." She reluctantly let go of his hand. The moon glow highlighted the hint of concern on his face. "I'm having a really nice time, but I think I need to take things slow. I'm hoping you're okay with that."

"I'm in no hurry." He took a step closer to her, pushing a loose strand of hair behind her ear. "I've got the patience of a saint."

"Good," she said, feeling her nerves relax as she looked at him. She didn't need to figure everything out right then. They were having a good time, and that's what mattered. Her eyes fell to his perfect smile as she imagined what it would be like to kiss him.

As if reading her mind, his hand cupped her face, his

tenderness melting her resolve. He leaned in, and his lips lightly grazed hers. Her mouth parted instinctively, inviting his tongue to meet hers. Their bodies drew closer together, deepening the kiss. Feeling his body against hers felt so right, so natural.

He pulled away, breaking the spell. "Sorry, I couldn't help it."

"That wasn't very saintly."

He smiled. "I have the patience of a saint, but I'm definitely no saint."

"Good."

He pulled her close again. "You're going to test my patience too, aren't you?"

"Of course," she said, and he laughed. "Although, I'm not very patient either, so we'll see what happens..." She wrapped her hands around his neck, and their bodies instinctively swayed with the trade winds.

"I look forward to that."

17

———

Adrian practically floated to the front door after Christian dropped her off. She replayed the heart-stopping kiss in her head, leaving a permanent smile on her face. The moment she turned the key in the door, reality came crashing down on her. Harold stood hyperventilating over her mother in the living room. "Help! Come quick!"

Margaret held her throat as she fought for air, her eyes bulged with fear. Her pale skin quickly turned various degrees of crimson, then violet. Adrian saw her mother's desperation for help, but her legs became pillars of concrete when she tried to move. Beads of sweat formed on her brow and her heart raced toward debilitating panic.

Finally finding the courage, she ran to her mother. She feared it would be the end and grabbed her mother's hand. "Call 911!" she barked at Harold, and he ran to the phone.

"Hang in there, Ma." Adrian stared into Margaret's fear-filled eyes, willing her to catch her breath. Adrian felt her mother's forehead. "She's burning up. Tell them she has a fever," she yelled to Harold.

"They said for her to push a finger into the indent above

her upper lip under her nose," he said. Adrian didn't give Margaret time to try it herself, immediately holding her finger against the spot with force, watching her mother's violet hue fade to crimson and then return to her normal color as she took a long, deep breath. She coughed as air filled her lungs. Tears of relief and fear pooled in the corners of her eyes.

"That worked!" Adrian squeezed Margaret, afraid to let go. Harold informed them an ambulance was on the way. "No protesting," Adrian said to Margaret, her voice shaky from adrenaline and a sad attempt at authority. "What were you doing anyway?"

"We were just sitting here watching TV, and I leaned in to kiss her, and I guess I caught her by surprise. I didn't mean to hurt her." He dipped his chin into his chest, shoving his hands in his pockets.

"Evening with the girls, huh, Ma?" Adrian raised an eyebrow. Margaret averted her gaze. "Well, thank God you were here," she said to Harold.

The ambulance arrived and swiftly took Margaret to the hospital. They didn't like the look of her vitals, her oxygen levels dangerously low. Adrian followed behind them with Harold, who refused to go home before knowing Margaret was going to be okay. Silence hung heavy between them, both lacking the energy for small talk with their mental energy focused on Margaret. What would have happened had Adrian not arrived home when she did? She shook her head, silencing that tiny, nagging voice. She couldn't give an ounce of energy to the thought, the repercussions too much to bear.

They rushed Margaret to some tests, and a nurse informed them it would be a few hours before they'd be able to see her. They set up camp in the stale, sterile waiting room. They weren't alone, sharing the space with a young Hispanic woman cradling a baby and a burly man with a thick gray beard holding his head in his hand. They opted for seats on the left side of the room with a clear view of a small television in the corner. An evangelist's tirade blared through the small speakers, advising anyone who'd listen to repent and accept the Lord as their Savior. Adrian bargained with the orange-faced buffoon in her head. *If I were to follow your advice, would my mother be spared?*

Harold rested his head against the wall and closed his eyes. Within minutes, he was snoring with his mouth wide open. Sleep wouldn't come as easily for Adrian, the room taut with fear and anxiety. She fidgeted, trying to tune out the sermon on the wall. Suddenly feeling claustrophobic, she decided to get some air. She headed toward her car to retrieve her cigarettes. She remembered her mother's hands waving across her body like Vanna White's, predicting the future like an ominous soothsayer. Adrian lit one anyway, taking a long drag. Predictions be damned. She watched her cigarette as the flame encompassed the paper and tobacco, turning it to ash.

She exhaled, watching the billows of smoke fade into the night. The silence did nothing to drown out the replay of her mother's fearful eyes as she gasped for air. Her adversarial mind raced with what ifs: What if she hadn't gotten home in time, what if her mother hadn't caught her breath? What if it had been the end? They still had so much unfinished business, so many things left to say. They'd still have a chance to settle things, right?

Tears streamed down her face. She wasn't ready to lose her mom, and she prayed to the God she knew to be real that it wouldn't be the end.

———

ADRIAN WOKE UP STARTLED, her phone buzzing in her pocket. She didn't recognize the number but decided to answer.

"Come get me."

"Mom?" She winced from pain, her muscles tense from sleeping in a bad position.

"Yes, come get me. Room 502." She hung up.

That was a hell of a wakeup call.

"I'll be right back," Adrian said to Harold, who rubbed sleep from his eyes.

The sun began its ascent, its powerful rays streaking through the windows and causing Adrian to shield her eyes. She searched for an elevator in the never-ending labyrinth of monochromatic sterility, starting to question if she were walking in circles. Why hasn't anyone thought to color code hospital wings, or have directories on the walls with big red dots showing you are here? She found an elevator that only went to the third floor and passed screaming babies in the maternity wing.

After passing many mothers in various stages of giving birth, she found an elevator going to the fifth floor. She squeezed into the corner of the elevator, sharing it with a nurse and a bed patient. The patient's IV drip swayed back and forth hypnotically, causing Adrian to almost miss her floor.

A number of nurses and hospital staff walked past her as if she were invisible. Clearly, they must be coming off the night shift, a changing of the guard commencing. She zigged, then zagged, finally finding her way to room 502. She peeked in to make sure.

Seeing her mother lying in the hospital bed made the severity of the situation all the more real. She looked so small, feeble, and defeated. Her pallid skin accentuated the dark circles under her eyes, which were glassy from lack of sleep. Adrian struggled to hide her reaction to seeing her mother look so powerless. This couldn't be the same woman who raised her, could it?

"Help me up." Margaret attempted to lift herself out of the hospital bed, still tethered by monitoring wires.

"Woah, lie back down." Adrian rushed to Margaret's side to stabilize her. "Shouldn't we wait for a doctor or something?" She looked around for someone to acknowledge them. Nurses rushed down the hallway, but none of them paid any attention to them.

"No, I'm done waiting. I'm ready to go." Margaret fiddled with her wire captors.

"Has a doctor seen you yet?"

"He's not going to tell me anything I don't already know. I have cancer, I'm dying, and staying here any longer isn't going to change that. I could die waiting at this point, so let's go." She yanked on some of the wires herself, creating a tangled mess.

Adrian acquiesced, assisting in setting her mother free. She knew better than anyone how stubborn Margaret could be, and she'd made up her mind. No use trying to talk her out of it. She untangled the wires, setting them aside one by one, and unhooked the cannula from her mother's nose before helping her out of bed. "Let me get you a wheelchair."

"I'm not an invalid." Margaret shuffled toward the doorway. Adrian held out a hand to help her and she waved it off. "Grab my clothes." She motioned to a stack of clothes perched on a chair.

Adrian looked at her mother's gown, gaping in the back. "Don't you want to change first?"

Margaret nodded, and Adrian helped her change back

into her street clothes. Margaret combed her fingers through her hair in an attempt to look presentable.

They headed toward the elevator. Adrian kept looking over her shoulder, trying to find someone to at least apologize to. On some level, she felt guilty, like she was busting a criminal out of jail. With no acknowledgment from any passers-by, she wondered if they'd become invisible. Had they somehow slipped through the cracks?

They took the elevator down to the main level, having somehow missed the labyrinth. As the doors opened, Adrian touched her mother's arm. "Are you sure we shouldn't wait for the doctor?"

"I'm done waiting. I'm tired, and I'm ready to go." Margaret shook her arm loose, her face brightening when Harold greeted her. He held out his arm for her to use as a crutch. He leaned over and gently kissed her head as they walked toward the exit.

Adrian paused, feeling like she should at least tell someone they were leaving. It had to be the most bizarre hospital visit she'd ever encountered.

"Adrian, go get the car."

She shrugged, following them out the sliding doors to drive them home.

———

ADRIAN PARKED the car in the driveway of her mother's house. She walked around to help her out of the passenger seat, Harold following suit. Margaret waved both of them off, insisting on doing it herself.

"Harold, I think she needs to rest, so you should go home."

As he opened his mouth to protest, Margaret cut him off. "I'll call you later, okay darling?" She kissed him on the cheek. For someone who'd just escaped a hospital, she still oozed confidence and femininity.

Adrian let her walk ahead, ready to catch her if she needed help. "You don't need to hover," Margaret said. When they crossed the threshold, she shuffled toward her usual chair in the living room.

"Don't you think you should lie down?"

She paused, then nodded, continuing her shuffle toward her bedroom door.

"Let me help you." Adrian held out her hand.

"I can do it myself."

Adrian hung back for a beat to fill a glass of water and retrieve Margaret's meds, letting her mother make her way into her room. A shoulder smacking into the door frame didn't faze her, but it made Adrian cringe. Margaret sat on the edge of the bed, and Adrian helped her get under the covers. She didn't even bother changing out of her clothes first.

Adrian handed her the pills and the water. She looked around her room, realizing it was the first time she'd been allowed into her mother's room. Margaret seemed to shrink in her queen-sized bed, the pale blue blankets enveloping her in a cocoon with ruffled pillow shams cradling her head. A picture of her and George sat next to a white lamp on her bedside table, and a mirror perched on top of a dresser on the opposite wall. She had a couple of pictures of her and the girls stuck in the mirror frame, and a maple jewelry box rested on top of a white doily covering the dresser. Adrian had no idea her mother was such a...girl.

As Margaret gulped water, something else caught Adrian's attention near the closet door. It looked like a small oxygen tank with a cannula attached, its long tube full of kinks after being shoved carelessly behind the pocket door. Adrian walked toward the closet, confirming her suspicion.

"Don't touch that!"

"Ma, what is this?" She pulled out part of the tube. Was she hiding her oxygen tank this whole time?

"It's nothing," she said, avoiding eye contact.

"Are you supposed to be wearing this?" Adrian felt nauseous with rage. What else was her mother hiding?

Margaret said nothing, staring at her daughter blankly.

"Answer me."

"No." She squirmed.

"You're lying." Adrian waited for her to come clean. The cat was out of the bag. But why wouldn't she wear it if she needed it? Adrian clenched her jaw. After all she'd done to help Margaret, did she even want to be helped? Was all of it for naught?

"You can go now."

"I'm not leaving until you put this on." She wheeled the portable tank over to the bedside. She held the cannula up to put it around her mother's head.

"Just leave me alone." Margaret blocked her hands.

"Do you have a death wish?" Adrian shook the plastic tubing at her.

"I'm dying anyway. What's the point?"

"You'll be more comfortable." Adrian attempted to loop the cannula around her mother.

"I don't care." She pushed her hands away.

"Stop it."

"No, you stop." Margaret pushed Adrian back with unexpected force, and she stumbled back, knocking over the picture of her parents before bracing herself against the wall. The frame shattered, glass spilling out in shards.

"What the hell?"

"Don't you talk to your mother that way."

"You're my mother? You could have fooled me. You're acting like a defiant brat!"

"Oh, please."

"Why won't you just wear your oxygen?"

"Because I don't want everyone to treat me differently!" Her outburst caught them both off-guard.

"What are you talking about?"

"I see the looks people give when they see old people in wheelchairs or wearing oxygen. I don't belong there. I don't need people taking pity on me."

Despite the tough words, Adrian saw fear in her mother's eyes. She may be sick, and she may be dying, but her mother's ego was very much still alive. She wasn't ready to let her dignity shatter, even if it meant being uncomfortable.

"They won't."

"Oh, please." She rolled her eyes.

"So, it's more important to you what other people think over being comfortable?" Adrian shook her head in disbelief. "That doesn't make any sense."

"Maybe to you it doesn't."

"What about what Harold thinks? Or Bev and Gilda? Or me?" Adrian paused for response. "Do none of us matter?"

"Pick up my picture."

"Don't dodge my question." Adrian placed the frame back on the bedside table. She felt tempted to use the oxygen herself, Margaret's stubbornness suffocating her. But she saw her mother's wheels turning as she calculated her response.

"If I agree to wear the oxygen around the house, will that appease you?"

"For now." Adrian looped the cannula around Margaret's head, placing it near her nose.

"That's all I'm agreeing to, just so we're clear."

"Okay, we'll see. Just get some rest." Adrian brushed hair off her mother's forehead, leaning down to kiss her third eye. She felt relieved, seeing her breathing more easily. "I'll check on you later." She turned off the bedside lamp and turned to look back from the doorway. Margaret looked peaceful, her eyes closed and already drifting toward sleep. Adrian couldn't believe she'd won a battle with her mother, but she knew the war was far from over.

18

Adrian closed the bedroom door softly behind her, leaving Margaret to nap. She still couldn't believe her mother had hidden the oxygen. What else could she be keeping secret? Adrian didn't understand why her mother wouldn't want to use something if it made her feel better. But one thing she'd learned about her mother over the years was she often behaved irrationally, especially when it came to her appearance and what others might think. Margaret held herself together no matter what. Even in the face of death, she insisted on putting on her makeup, keeping up appearances while her body betrayed her. God forbid she take her last breath sans mascara.

Adrian seized the opportunity to call Laura and sneak a cigarette. She needed her best friend to help her make sense of everything. Before she could dial the number, her phone rang. Christian's number popped up on her caller ID. "Is everything okay?"

"Yeah, as good as it can be, I guess." Adrian rubbed her forehead. "How'd you know?"

"Aunt Bev told me what happened."

"Oh." Harold must have told the girls. Silence hung between them for a few moments.

"What can I do to help?"

"I'm not sure." What was Adrian doing? If the last few hours told her anything, there was no way she could consider getting romantically involved with someone right then. Maybe she needed to make a clean break. The timing was all wrong.

"Adrian?"

She sighed. "Actually, can we push pause on whatever this is for a little while? I really need to give my full attention to my mom right now."

"Yeah...sure."

A pit formed in Adrian's stomach. She really didn't want to do it, but she also didn't see any other choice. "I'll call you soon, okay? Promise." She hung up and stared at the black screen. Was pushing him away really the right thing to do? She'd had such a good time on their date, and things felt so natural with him. She hadn't experienced a connection quite like that before, not even with Brad. He seemed very understanding and patient, so why couldn't they take things at a snail's pace?

But if she'd learned anything in the last twelve hours, it was that life was fragile, and her mother's time was running out. She wanted to make the most of what little time remained and dating Christian would interfere with that. She'd never forgive herself if she missed seeing her mother take her last breath, out having the time of her life with Christian while her mother's ended. Her mother needed her, and she knew deep down she needed her too.

Before stewing any longer, she dialed Laura's number. As it rang, she lit a cigarette pursed between her lips. She thought about her mother struggling to breathe, and it made her lose the desire to smoke. She threw the cigarette away as Laura answered. "Hey girl! How was your date?"

"Well, our date was great," she said, guilt punching her in the gut. "But I just brought my mother home from the hospital."

"What happened?"

Adrian told her all the details, from finding Margaret on the couch choking to rushing her to the hospital.

"Wow, I'm so sorry."

"Yeah, me too." She choked up.

"How long does she have?"

"No clue. She told me to come get her from her room, and we left before we saw the doctor."

"She literally walked out? Is that even possible?"

"Apparently, it is. She'd been waiting for a long time to be seen, and she said she was tired of waiting. She didn't want to wait to hear what she already knew, and I guess they were slammed with other patients. You know how she can be."

"Weird." Silence hung heavy between them. "Are you okay?"

Tears formed at the corners of her eyes. "Not really."

"Do you want me to come? I'll jump in the car, or fly, or—"

"No, it's okay. I need you to sell my house," Adrian said. "Speaking of that, any progress there?"

"Actually, I was going to call you about that." Her voice sank. "Title notified me someone recently filed a lis pendens against the house."

"What does that mean?"

"Basically, someone filed this encumbrance to establish their interest in the property. Know anyone who would do that?" she asked, her tone one of knowing.

"It has to be Celeste."

"Yeah, that's what I'm thinking too, so you might want to tell your new lawyer about this."

Adrian shrugged. "I guess I don't have a choice."

"Don't worry. We'll get through this."

"I hope you're right."

"And speaking of lawyers, what's up with you and Christian?"

"Nothing," Adrian replied. "I told him now isn't a good time with everything going on with my mom and now this lis-whatever you called it."

Laura paused. "You know it's okay to be happy, right?"

"I know."

"You just have to give yourself permission. It doesn't make you a bad daughter or widow or whatever your mind is thinking."

"But what about this paternity thing? How would it look if I were gallivanting around town with a new boyfriend when the dirt has barely settled on Brad's grave?"

"Who's looking? I guarantee no one will care as much as you think they will."

Adrian considered her words. "Maybe you're right."

"You know I am."

"Maybe." Adrian smiled.

Laura chuckled. "Let me know what Brian says about the encumbrance."

"I will. Love you."

"Love you more."

––––––––

ADRIAN WAITED in the lobby for her new lawyer, Brian, to wrap up his other meeting. Her mind cycled through thoughts of her mother, Christian, and Brad's love child, too powerful to attempt any distraction tactics. Did Celeste really file the encumbrance? What recourse did Adrian have? What would Celeste be entitled to if, in fact, that was Brad's baby she carried? She was so close to finally living out her dream of being an artist, and the thought of having it ripped away made her nauseous.

On the plus side, at least Margaret was living up to her promise, wearing her oxygen around the house. She still refused to wear it in public, and there was a big difference in her energy when she didn't use it. Margaret must have felt a difference, since she started wearing the oxygen without a reminder. Maybe she'd cave and start wearing it full-time, strangers' odd looks and opinions be damned. One day at a time.

Adrian crossed her legs and pulled a floral wrap dress over her knee, wedge heel dangling as she fidgeted. She wanted to look nice for a probable run-in with Christian, but a sleeveless dress was a bad choice given it was winter inside the office. She teetered back and forth on changing her mind, feeling stupid for pumping the brakes so soon. But with everything going on, it just wasn't the right time. She needed to put her attention on her mother and figuring out the next move with Celeste.

"Brian will see you now," the receptionist said. They walked past Christian's office and she peered in, hoping to see him. Her heart sank a little when his office was empty. Maybe she'd catch him on the way out.

The receptionist held the door open to Brian's office, and Adrian noticed it was more traditional than Christian's. His grand cherry wood desk and hefty leather chairs made the space feel small, reminding her of an old smoking room where gentlemen retire after dinner.

Brian stood to shake her hand, his big meaty claws nearly crushing her bony fingers. His steel blue eyes were surprisingly warm but had an edge to them. He was broad and tall, with sandy blond hair perfectly parted to the side and a meticulously manicured beard. He appeared to be in his mid-50s, affirmed by a picture of his family hanging prominently on the wall, which included a beautiful wife, three sons and their wives, and five grandchildren. They exchanged pleasantries, and he wasted no time diving in. "You were right, I did find out it was Celeste Robinson who filed the lis pendens on your house." He leafed through paper in a manila folder. "Have you gone through probate yet?"

Adrian shook her head.

"I was afraid of that." He grimaced. "Were you planning on it?"

"I didn't see the need, given the fact that we shared everything."

"Well, I'm afraid you no longer have a choice. She's forcing your hand, so to speak."

"So, what are my options?" Adrian shifted in her seat.

"First things first. In order for her to file this lis pendens, she needs to have proof of her supposed interest. I've requested this proof be provided so we can evaluate it."

"What kind of proof? Like the baby?"

"No, not quite. Since the baby isn't born yet, she needs to provide other proof, like text messages, emails, that sort of thing, to show enough proof that the child is his...allegedly."

Adrian's body shook as adrenaline coursed through her veins. She didn't want to see proof like that in black and white. A baby was already a lot to handle but seeing the exchange of printed words between Brad and another woman made Adrian feel sick. She didn't want to re-open old wounds, the scabs having just fallen off on her path to healing. "Will I have to read it?"

"No, I guess not. But I will, since that's my job." He forced a smile.

"And what if signs point to her child being his?"

"We won't know anything for certain until we do the paternity test. But if we discover the child is his when all is said and done, Celeste and the baby would be entitled to a portion of Brad's estate, which would be determined through probate."

"How large of a percentage are we talking about?" Adrian braced herself for the worst.

"It would most likely be a third but could be more or less, depending on probate."

A third? "How long does probate usually take?"

He grimaced. "It could take up to a year in a case like this."

A year? She felt sucker punched, staring blankly at his desk as words escaped her.

He closed the file and plopped his meaty hand on top of hers. "I know this is tough, but the silver lining is that we still don't have the paternity test results. Anything could happen."

"She seemed pretty convinced it's Brad's child she's carrying." Adrian pulled away and crossed her arms. "She's probably telling the truth."

"I wouldn't be so sure. Haven't you ever watched daytime TV?"

She laughed. "You and Christian are definitely partners." He gave her a confused look. "He said the exact same thing to me."

"What can I say?" He shrugged. "Great minds, I suppose."

She nodded, thinking of Christian.

"Hang in there, kiddo. I'll do everything I can to find out the truth and come to amenable terms."

"I certainly hope so."

REELING after her meeting with Brian, Adrian stopped by Christian's office. She needed to see a friendly face after the news she'd heard, and her heart sank when his office still stood empty. She thought about how safe she felt in his arms the other night, and she wanted to feel something, anything, other than the dread sitting in her stomach from her meeting.

"Where's Christian?" she asked the receptionist.

"Right here." She turned around to see him, and her heart caught in her throat. His charcoal gray wool suit was perfectly tailored to his muscular body, the smell of his cologne intoxicating. He'd opted for no tie, his crisp white shirt unbuttoned just enough to see the top of his smooth chest. His hazel eyes locked on hers, and he swallowed hard. Seeing him sparked an urge within her, and she couldn't hold back any longer.

"Can I see you in your office, please?" She tried her best to conceal her sudden desire. He guided her into the office, his touch on her back lighting her skin on fire. He closed the door behind them.

"Is everything o—"

She pressed her lips against his. Surprise wore off quickly, and his mouth met hers with the same passionate intensity. His hands rose to frame her face as their tongues slow danced together. Her hands roamed over his shoulders and chest until she found the row of buttons on the shirt concealing his flesh. She made quick work of them, and his hands lowered to her waist, grazing her butt as he pulled her dress over her head.

He looked down at her with lust in his eyes. "You are so beautiful," he murmured, and she smiled as her mouth met his again.

She gripped his biceps as he carried her over to the desk, her legs naturally wrapping around his waist. He cleared a space for them and gently laid her down. She reached to unbutton his pants, freeing his desire. He slid her panties to the side and they quickly became one, parts of her buzzing with life after being dormant for so long.

Merging with Christian was spiritual, carnal, and everything she needed to feel. He somehow knew her body so well, like they had been lovers for years. He stifled their moans by kissing her as they reached their peaks together. They slowly descended the mountain of lust they had climbed together, neither one of them wanting to break the physical connection.

"That was...wow," he said, catching his breath.

All she could muster in return was a very descriptive, intelligent *yeah* in agreement. He buried his head against her shoulder, nuzzling her neck. His light kisses sent ripples of pleasure throughout her body in perfect sync with the aftershock of her climax.

They reluctantly helped each other put themselves back together. As she helped him button his last button, he pulled her in and pressed his lips to hers. She wanted nothing more than to stay like that, in his arms, feeling intoxicated with every kiss.

He pulled away and looked at his watch. "I'd love to keep doing this, but I have an appointment in a few minutes. Call you later?"

She nodded. "Okay." He kissed her softly on the forehead. She adjusted the hem of her dress before he opened his office door. They said goodbye, and she had to avoid eye contact with anyone, afraid her face would give away the nature of their meeting.

On the drive home, she couldn't erase the smile from her face. Christian made her feel different, more alive somehow, than she'd felt in years. The euphoria of their merging sent aftershock waves through her body. She could get used to that. Despite bad timing, she couldn't imagine not seeing where things could go. What they had was special, worth exploring again and again.

I hope he feels the same way.

When she arrived at her mother's house, it was eerily quiet, and Margaret's door was shut. Maybe she'd decided to take a nap. Everything was taking more of a toll on her body these days. Adrian quietly thanked God for helping her avoid an awkward post-coital conversation with her mother.

She went to the kitchen for a glass of water, skipping the ice in fear of waking Margaret. She gulped, replaying Christian's tenderness over in her mind. He had become a wonderful surprise in so many ways in the last few weeks, and regardless of whatever happened next, she'd—

"I'll be right back, my sweet," a man's voice said, shutting a door behind him. Adrian's eyes grew wide with panic, and she felt frozen in place as Harold rounded the corner and shrieked. He stood paralyzed in the doorway, which perfectly framed him in her mother's pink bathrobe, overflowing with a forest of salt and pepper chest hair. "What are you doing here?"

"I could ask the same of you, but I really don't want to know." Her face burned as she tried to stifle laughter.

He pulled her mother's robe a little closer to his body, trying to conceal the chest hair. "Could you tell me where to find the water glasses?"

"Right here." She pulled two from the cupboard and handed them over. He mumbled thanks while avoiding all eye contact. She watched him fill both glasses with water and scurry away. He turned to face her before leaving the kitchen. His mouth opened and then quickly shut. He bolted toward Margaret's bedroom, slamming the door behind him. She strained to hear their soft voices, and her mother let out an embarrassed shriek. Adrian couldn't hold back any longer, giggling as she refilled her glass.

This was definitely a first. She hadn't seen her mother with anyone other than her father and didn't think she'd ever be in that situation. She couldn't help feeling like a parental figure, busting her mother after her afternoon delight. She realized how much Margaret had surprised her in the time she'd been there, and how much she still had to discover about her while she could.

19

That was hot. Christian had to catch his breath. If anyone told him he would christen his office with the girl he'd pined after for years in high school, he would have laughed in their face. He would have looked around for cameras because he was being pranked. But that definitely wasn't a dream. In fact, it was so much better than he'd ever imagined. They'd fit together perfectly, like she was the missing piece all along. He wanted to put them together over and over again.

He took a deep breath, still descending the mountain of lust he'd climbed with Adrian. He had to admit, that wasn't what he was accustomed to when a girl said she wanted to take things slow. Was what just happened between them the right move? Was he being tested, and if so, did he fail by not showing restraint? The way she'd looked in her dress and the way she'd kissed him—there was no way he could have shown any even if he'd tried.

But what now?

He shouldn't overthink it. Clearly, she wanted him just as badly. It had been so long since he'd felt that way about anyone, and he wasn't about to let her go. Even if they moved at a slower pace from then on, he knew with total certainty she was worth it.

With his heart beat finally slowing to normal, he put the contents of his desk back together. It might be better to let her take the lead and set the pace. She'd taken charge that afternoon and it had turned out well for both of them, so she wouldn't steer them wrong. Whatever she was comfortable with worked for him.

Once everything was in place, he had just enough time to check his email and review his notes before his next meeting. He sorted through the typical junk and deleted most of it, but a message from a name he hadn't seen in a while popped up on his screen. One he never thought he'd see again.

What does she want?

He considered moving it to junk as well, because no good could come from opening that message. But of course, curiosity got the best of him, and his hand betrayed him, double-clicking to open it, revealing its contents.

From: Sarah Nelson

Subject: (blank)

I need to talk to you. Can we meet?

Many expletives came to mind, but what didn't was any logical explanation as to why she chose to reach out. Her timing was terrible or impeccable, depending on the point of view. Did she have some kind of ex-girlfriend alarm that went off, saying, "Hey, your ex is happy. You should go ruin it now"?

Old wounds threatened to burst open as he read her words over again. What could she possibly have to say to him after all the time they'd been apart? Maybe he was jumping to conclusions. Maybe she needed legal advice or something else unrelated to their relationship. But still, whatever her reason was, it couldn't be good.

"Christian, your three o'clock is here," Deidre said through the intercom function of his phone.

"Okay, please send them in."

Saved by the bell. He'd have to wait until later to decide how to handle Sarah.

———

ADRIAN HAD a looming sense of dread as she made breakfast. After sleeping on what she'd done the day before with Christian, she'd decided it was a mistake. A very fun mistake, but a mistake, nonetheless. Had she ruined what they had started to build by rushing into sex? He hadn't called her when she thought he might, which only proved her right. So, what now?

She liked him a lot and really enjoyed the time they'd spent together. But was she ready to jump into another relationship? It didn't stop her from acting on physical impulses, which only left her with a pit of regret in her stomach the morning after. But in reality, she'd just ended a marriage, and her heart needed time to heal before beating for another man.

She wanted to talk to Laura but wasn't sure if telling her what happened was wise. She already knew Laura would say, "There are no accidents." If she was right, it would work out in the end. But how did Adrian want things to work out?

She heard her mother stirring and started preparing oatmeal with raisins and brown sugar. Margaret shuffled into the kitchen, and Adrian grabbed a mug from the cabinet and filled it with coffee, placing it in front of her as she sat at the table. Margaret acknowledged her with a nod of appreciation, and Adrian stirred the oats on the stovetop.

Her mother was quiet. Harold left sometime the night before, and Adrian had avoided any common areas of the house in fear of seeing him in the pink robe again or hearing sounds she couldn't un-hear. She was still surprised at her mother's behavior. She'd never known Margaret to be with any man except George, so that alone was a shock. But was her mother acting responsible given her health?

She finished with the oats and placed them on the table, sitting in her usual spot. Margaret mumbled a simple thanks, avoiding eye contact with her daughter. Adrian sipped her coffee, watching the morning dew begin to burn off in the light of day. She looked at her mother out of the corner of her eye. Who would be the first to speak? Someone needed to address the elephant in the room.

"You really don't have anything to say?"

"About what?" Margaret mumbled.

"My run-in with Harold in the kitchen yesterday."

"What about it?"

"Is that really something you should be doing in your...condition?"

Margaret put down her spoon, looking pointedly at her daughter. "What condition?"

Adrian paused, calculating a response under her mother's intense glare. "I think, given your health, your actions yesterday were irresponsible."

"Oh, for Pete's sake. Is this about your father?"

"What—no, this is about you. What if you died or couldn't catch your breath or—"

"Then I'd have gone out with a smile on my face."

"Ma, really. I can't believe you just said that to me."

"What? I'm sorry if my being a woman is a shock to you, Adrian, but I don't see why you're upset."

"Because you could have stopped breathing."

"At some point, I will. How I choose to spend the time I have left and with whom is my decision."

"But shouldn't you do whatever you can to prolong your life?"

"So, I should be afraid to live because I'm dying? What's the point of that?"

Margaret's words hit Adrian hard. She wasn't sure how to respond or how to express to Margaret she wasn't ready for her to go yet. She fought back tears.

Margaret reached across the table, setting her hand on top of Adrian's. "It's not news to anyone that I'm dying. I don't have any control over when or how it will happen, but the one thing I do have control over is how I spend the rest of the time I have. And while that clock is ticking, I'm going to live how I see fit. Got it?"

Adrian nodded. "Okay."

"Good." Margaret squeezed her hand before letting it go to take a sip of coffee. "Besides, your judgment isn't good for my...condition."

Adrian rolled her eyes. "Whatever."

Margaret smirked. "Oh, come on. Lighten up."

Adrian's tough exterior started to crack. She began to smile, then stopped. "You done?" She motioned to her mother's half-eaten oatmeal, and Margaret nodded. Adrian cleared the table and did the dishes.

"How was your meeting yesterday?" Margaret asked.

Adrian turned off the faucet, feeling her ears turn red. She knew mothers always had a certain *knowing* about them, but there was no way she could have known what happened. "Meeting?"

"With your new lawyer?"

"Oh, that meeting." She recounted the detail of the lis pendens and the probability of exhuming Brad's body for paternity when the time came.

"Wow, that's...intense."

Adrian finished the dishes and topped off her mug. "Would you like more coffee?" she offered.

Margaret shook her head. "Did you have another meeting yesterday?"

"No, why?"

"Because you asked which meeting I was talking about."

Adrian shrugged. "Need more coffee, I suppose."

Margaret wasn't buying it. "Doesn't Christian work with him?"

Adrian blushed. "Yeah, so?"

"Huh. I thought so."

"What?"

"Nothing."

Adrian felt her face turn a brighter shade of red as she mumbled something about going to take a shower. She needed to get out of there before her face gave away any more detail.

———

ADRIAN AWOKE with a burst of creative energy that couldn't be contained. She made coffee to-go, her creative forces alive and firing on all cylinders. She'd had the idea for a painting for a while, and it felt like the right time to bring it to life. Knowing her mother's light would soon burn out in the world, it only made sense to commemorate her existence. The idea of painting Margaret's crossing over to the next phase in her journey, to a place where only love exists, warmed Adrian's heart. She hoped her mother would appreciate it too.

While things were still a little strained, they were chiseling away at the walls between them. Adrian had begun to see her mother as a woman first and a mother second, which helped bring forth new levels of understanding.

While she didn't agree with her mother's denial of treatment or fight, Adrian had to find a way to accept her decisions. They'd spent years with tension between them, and it never changed anything. The last thing she wanted to do was fight during whatever time they had left.

She quickly set up her board, paints, and pencil, ready to sketch her idea to life. She scribbled with intensity, capturing every detail. She paused a few times, assessing the accuracy of her sketch against the image in her mind's eye.

Once content, she prepped her paints, mixing a couple of them together to get the right shades. Once ready, she painted with desperation and fervor. As her hand glided across the canvas, it felt like it was being guided by an outside force. Maybe her dad was there, helping her make it perfect. She'd likely finish the painting just in time for group. Would Christian be there?

A week had passed since their merger in his office, and he hadn't called. Given the intensity between them, the static of dead air surprised her. Maybe he was turned off by her aggression, or maybe he was trapped under his desk, physically unable to reach his phone to dial for help. She shook her head at the irrational thought. Maybe he wasn't who she thought he was. Besides, how much did she know about him? And Brad had certainly been an example of people not always being who they seemed to be.

Although Christian had proved himself to be different. Christian was other-worldly hot and always said the right things. Was the chemical reaction between them only in Adrian's head? Maybe she'd gone crazy since moving back home. Could it be that she'd fabricated the whole experience, desperate for a distraction from her mother? Oh, who was she kidding? She knew what they'd experienced was real. Very real.

But why hadn't he called?

She considered being the bigger person and calling him herself. After all, she'd made the bold move in his office, so why did picking up the phone seem colossal? It was the twenty-first century, after all. She'd always pursued whatever she wanted, letting nothing stand in her way. But for some reason, this felt different. At the risk of seeming old-fashioned, Adrian wanted to be pursued. And dammit, Christian should want to pursue her.

Maybe the lack of communication was the Universe's way of saying it wasn't the right time, or the right guy, to trust with her heart. The last time she gave her heart to someone, he cheated. Besides, she still had big messes to clean up from her marriage. Was it really smart to get involved with someone new?

She put her brush down, feeling confusion and frustration begin to infiltrate the painting. Even with the brevity of their relationship (if it could be called that), she felt disappointed things didn't work out the way she'd envisioned with Christian. On the bright side, she'd probably see him at group. Then she'd get answers.

———

ADRIAN ARRIVED at group hoping to see Christian, but he was not there. She knew he tended to cut it close, barely making it every time the group met, so there was still time for him to show up.

She grabbed a Styrofoam cup and filled it with water before making her way over to Karen. "So, you survived the fall. How was it?"

"Oh, it was—what a life changing experience," Karen mused. "Although I don't see how you said it was calm up there. I was scared to death the whole time." She laughed nervously.

Adrian smiled. "That's normal. The real question is, would you do it again?"

Karen pondered. "You know, it might sound crazy, but yeah, I think I would."

"Good for you. Actually, what do you think about us planning a group trip? We could all go together."

"Absolutely not," Susan said, joining them. "There's no way you're getting me to jump out of a perfectly good airplane."

"Oh, come on. It could be the ultimate trust exercise." Adrian grinned.

"Where's your sense of adventure?" Henry teased, pulling up a chair.

"If that's adventurous, I'm at peace with being lame," Susan said.

Adrian laughed, and Karen had everyone find their seats, signifying it was time to do some work. "Today, I thought we might spend some time talking about practicing the present," Karen said. "We all have memories of loved ones that draw us to the past, but it's important to find peace, move forward with our lives, and make the most of what we still have while we still have it. At first, it might feel like we're betraying our loved ones by not continuously honoring their memory, but what about practicing self-care and honoring ourselves? It's important to stay present, since we all know firsthand how fragile life is and that it can be gone in an instant. Does anyone have a particular way they practice staying present despite the past pulling you back?"

Adrian looked around, waiting for someone to speak. She had to admit she was having a hard time practicing the present, wondering where Christian was. "Actually," she surprised herself as she spoke. "I'm struggling with this, to be honest. I'm sure you all remember from my previous outburst that my husband died in a car accident, almost taking me with him. And what's strange is that, through his death, I learned my mother is dying from stage four lung cancer, complicated by COPD."

"Wow, I'm so sorry," Karen said, reaching over to place her hand on Adrian's. Susan nodded her head in agreement.

Adrian nodded her acknowledgement before continuing. "When Brad died, I moved back here to take care of my mother, and to say our relationship has been strained is a severe understatement. But she's forgoing treatment for her condition, and I'm having a hard time understanding why she's giving up."

"You have no choice but to stay present," Susan said. "When Paul got pancreatic cancer, he also decided to forgo treatment. I didn't understand why, but he told me it wasn't worth it to spend his last days sick from chemo, knowing he was going to die anyway. I didn't agree, but I honored his wishes, and the last three months we had together were the sweetest we'd had in our thirty years of marriage. We lived and loved like every day was his last because it was entirely possible that it could have been."

Karen handed her a box of tissues, and Susan rolled her eyes before taking one. "Of course, the new girl gets me to crack." She dabbed her eyes and laughed.

"You're a strong woman, Susan, and I admire your courage in letting your guard down with us," Karen said.

"The same applies to you," Susan said to Adrian. "Do whatever you can to be present with your mom and accept her wishes for her last days. You never know when it will actually be the last. You don't want any regrets."

Adrian considered the words, knowing Susan was right. She needed to accept that her mother had made her choice about how to spend her last days. Now Adrian had a choice on how to spend that time with her, and she knew she didn't want to fight anymore. "Thank you," she said to Susan. They smiled at one another.

"Well, I've been more present in my life and I'm happy to say I've lost five pounds," Gina said. "I know it's not much, but it's the most progress I've made in the last year."

"That's wonderful, dear." Henry reached over to give her a sideways hug.

"Excellent," Karen said. "I wouldn't mind losing a little weight myself. What's your secret?" Karen didn't need to lose anything but was doing what she did best—going out of her way to make someone feel accepted for exactly who and how they were.

"I don't know, something just clicked in me that Trudy would want me to take care of myself. I've been walking every evening after dinner, and it's helped me avoid eating dessert."

"Ugh, I'm such a sucker for dessert," Karen mused. "I can't say no to anything sweet."

"Dark chocolate," Susan said. "The darker the better."

"Nah, buttercream cookies," Henry said. "The ones that come in that blue tin."

"What about wedding cake?" Frank asked. "That's always been my weakness."

"You all lost me at dessert," Adrian said. "Give me salty, like smothered cheese fries with bacon." She rubbed her stomach.

"Just as we were beginning to like you," Susan said.

They all laughed, and for the first time since she'd arrived, Adrian finally felt like she'd found her place in her hometown.

20

On the drive home, Adrian dialed Laura. She picked up after several rings, sounding out of breath. "Everything okay?"

"Yeah, everything's fine. What's up?" Laura attempted nonchalance and failed.

"You sound out of breath. Can you talk?"

"Sure, I've got a minute." Dylan screamed in the background.

"If now isn't a good time..."

"Yes, it's fine. He's just refusing to eat, which is making Mommy crazy." Her tone bordered on maniacal.

"Why don't we just catch up later?"

"Okay." Laura sounded relieved. "But do you mind stopping by my mom's house this afternoon? She has a little something for you."

"Of course. Is she home now?"

"Yeah, she should be." Dylan wailed in the background, making Adrian cringe. They said their goodbyes and hung up.

Adrian changed course and headed toward Laura's parents' house, which was only about fifteen minutes away.

She felt a little embarrassed it had taken her so long to visit them. Better late than never, right?

As she pulled up and parked by the curb, she noticed how little their home had changed. The stucco exterior was a warm shade of beige, and white trim made the windows pop. A sago palm fanned its fronds like a proud peacock, not to be outdone by the large live oak blanketing the front yard. The driveway comprised of stone pavers, and a warm wooden garage door replaced the old metal one that was peppered with dents from Laura's dad's putting practice. Memories of sleepovers, dinners, and birthday parties flooded Adrian's inner screen. She'd practically lived there in her youth, it being their preferred gathering place.

Laura's mother, Elizabeth, was the epitome of a mother in Adrian's mind: warm, nurturing, and encouraging. Adrian often felt jealous of Laura's close relationship with her mother, wishing she and Margaret could have a bond like theirs. But they were different people, and she had to appreciate her relationship with Margaret for what it was.

Adrian knocked on the door, and Elizabeth answered. "I was wondering when you'd show up," she said, leaning in for a long, warm hug. When she pulled back, Adrian admired her. Elizabeth's ash brown hair was neatly pulled up into a bun, and she looked ten years younger than her age. Her mahogany eyes beamed with pride and excitement, and she smelled of cookies and roasted chicken. She wore an old apron yellowed with age, peppered with many indiscernible spots and Never Trust A Skinny Cook stamped in faded block letters across the front. It made Adrian smile, since Laura's mother was anything but pudgy.

"Come in, I'm just baking cookies."

"You're still like Mrs. Cleaver, I see."

"Oh, stop." She playfully patted Adrian's arm. A kitchen timer went off and Elizabeth hurried after it.

The kitchen had received a face lift. The dark oak cabinets were painted a light shade of gray, and white marble countertops replaced the peeling buttercream Formica. Elizabeth offered her a glass of water, and she sat at a bar stool near their kitchen island just like old times.

They made small talk while Elizabeth took a batch of cookies out of the oven and prepped another cookie sheet. Adrian's mouth watered as the scent of confectionary perfection tickled her nose. "Paul is out playing golf this afternoon. He's going to be so sorry he missed you."

"There will be other times. I promise," Adrian said.

After placing the new cookie sheet in the oven, Elizabeth wrinkled her brow as she studied Adrian. "Something's bothering you." She held a hand to Adrian's forehead. "Man trouble?" Elizabeth always had a sixth sense about things. "Oh, what am I thinking? How's your mother?"

"She's okay, I guess." Adrian shrugged. "We're just taking it one day at a time."

"I know this can't be easy, and I'm here for you and Margaret. Whatever you need."

"Thanks." Adrian noticed a hint of regret in her eyes when she mentioned her mother.

"I think we need to try one of these cookies, don't you?" Elizabeth smiled.

Adrian nodded. "I thought you'd never ask."

Elizabeth handed her a warm cookie. "Did Laura tell you what I found?"

"No," she mumbled. "Should I be worried?"

"Of course not." Elizabeth giggled, finished her cookie, and wiped her hands on the apron. "Let's go into the living room. I have something to show you." She looked at the clock, nodding her head. "But first, let's get something a little stronger than water and a cookie, shall we?" She pulled a bottle of white wine from the fridge. "Want a spritzer?"

Adrian nodded, cracking a smile at Elizabeth living dangerously, breaking out the wine before a socially acceptable time of day. She made quick work of making their drinks before they moved into the living room. They sat together on a faded blue plaid couch, and Elizabeth pulled two coasters from the corner of the rustic oak coffee table for their drinks. Laura was practically with them in the form of family portraits lining the mantle of the hardly used fireplace. Why they even built homes with fireplaces in Florida was a total mystery.

Elizabeth leaned over and grabbed a brown photo album barely held together with duct tape, pages poking out in different directions. "I was going through some old boxes in the garage last week and came across some pictures I thought you might like to see." She carefully opened the album, and they looked through photos of Laura and Adrian as children celebrating birthdays and silly pictures of them playing dress-up—Laura in her father's cowboy boots that came up to her waist and Adrian clogging along clumsily in Elizabeth's stilettos. They both laughed at the memories as they viewed each image, a tiny window into good times long passed.

Elizabeth turned the page, revealing pictures of her and a woman who looked remarkably like Margaret. Her head was leaned back in laughter, and Elizabeth was next to her. This had to have been before she was born. "Is that...?"

"Yes." Elizabeth grabbed her hand. "I thought you'd like to see these pictures. Did you know Margaret and I were good friends?"

"I vaguely remember." Adrian searched her memory, unable to recall a time when her mother looked so full of joy. "This looks like it was before I was born."

"It was. Your mother and I were pretty tight for a while." Her eyes rueful, Adrian waited for her to say more. Instead, she turned to another page in the album, revealing a photo of Margaret full of bliss, holding a giggling baby up in the air.

"Is that me?" Adrian asked, and Elizabeth nodded. Her mother looked proud, practically buoyant, a stark contrast to who she had known her to be. "I've never seen my mother so happy."

"You know she loves you." Elizabeth placed her hand on Adrian's, searching her face for comprehension. "I know she has a funny way of showing it sometimes, but that's never changed."

Adrian swallowed hard, feeling deep-rooted emotions bubbling to the surface. "She certainly does." She couldn't remember the last time her mother said she loved her. Had she ever? Deep down, Adrian knew it, but sometimes, it'd be nice to hear.

"She's never been good with words," Elizabeth said, as if reading Adrian's mind. "But one thing's for sure—she's always wanted nothing but the best for you."

"Do you still talk?"

"No," She grimaced, "And I've been thinking about going to see her. We should put our differences in the past behind us."

"What happened?"

"We had a disagreement. About you, actually." Elizabeth took a big sip of her spritzer. "I always thought she was too hard on you. Too critical. She wanted to be closer to you and couldn't understand why you favored your father. I said some things in honesty, trying to help her as a mother and my friend, and I guess she didn't really want to hear them." She shrugged. "Afterward, she pulled away, and I tried to apologize, but she wouldn't hear it. We've never been the same since. You of all people know how she's always right." She forced a smile.

So, her mother's critical nature wasn't only in Adrian's head. Other people saw it too. She still didn't understand why Margaret was so hard on her, and she secretly wondered if she even wanted to have a child. Adrian remember her speaking fondly about her budding career before Adrian came along. Had she ruined her mother's life?

She looked down at the photo. Seeing her mother so full of joy holding her in the air certainly made it seem like Adrian was wanted and loved. While seeing the photos and hearing what Elizabeth shared helped fill in some gaps, she couldn't help feeling a little confused. In front of her was evidence of a softer side of Margaret that Adrian had long forgotten about, and recently, little glimmers made brief appearances. Could anything be done to fully unearth it?

"Thank you for sharing all of this with me. It's actually helped me make sense of some things."

Elizabeth pulled the picture of Margaret and baby Adrian from the album. "I think you should hang onto this one."

Adrian held the picture in her hand, feeling sparks of the reconnection with Margaret she'd longed for since her arrival. "Thanks, I definitely will."

———

ADRIAN STOOD in the kitchen over a pot of golden milk about to boil over, lost in thought about the afternoon. She appreciated Elizabeth showing her the old photos but felt more confused after seeing them. She recalled the picture of her and her mother in her mind's eye, seeing the sheer joy on Margaret's face. Adrian searched her mind for the catalyst that caused Margaret to change and came up short. Obviously, Elizabeth saw it too, or she wouldn't have said anything. And if she and Margaret used to be close, Adrian wondered why her mother would react so poorly to her concern and push her away.

She had a hard time believing Elizabeth about her mother being jealous of Adrian's relationship with her father and how she longed to be closer to her daughter. If it was true, she had a funny way of showing it. Was she that unaware of the effect of her criticisms? In contrast, Adrian's father was warm and encouraging. No wonder she'd favored him.

"Are you trying to burn the house down?" Margaret said, turning off the burner. The contents in the pot quickly settled to a slow boil before reaching a state of calm.

"Sorry." Adrian shook her head, snapping out of it. She reached for two mugs before realizing her mother had beaten her to it.

"Are you okay?"

"Yeah," Adrian lied, filling the mugs.

Margaret examined her daughter. "Oh, I see what's going on."

"What?"

"Christian hasn't called you, has he?"

Adrian's jaw dropped, and she quickly shut it. How did her mother know about Christian? Before she could answer, Margaret motioned for them to sit at the dining table.

"So, tell me what's on your mind." Margaret blew on her milk, her mouth a perfect O.

"I saw Elizabeth today."

She stopped blowing, her body tense. "Oh? How is she doing?"

"Good. Said she wants to come visit with you sometime."

"Pay her respects while she still can, huh?"

Adrian shrugged. "I wasn't aware you two used to be so close."

"That was a long time ago." She avoided eye contact, staring into her cup. She shifted uncomfortably and adjusted her cannula.

"We went through some old photo albums."

"Wow, she really is feeling nostalgic."

Adrian pulled the photograph Elizabeth gave her out of her purse, placing it on the table facing her mother. "She's not the only one."

Margaret softened as she studied the photograph. She held it between her bony fingers. "I remember that day." She smiled. "I'm glad she found this one." She set it down, patting it with approval.

Adrian swallowed hard. She knew it was now or never, and she might lose the nerve if she didn't just ask what she'd been thinking the entire afternoon. Nay, her entire life. "Ma, did you want me?" Her voice cracked and she blushed, feeling stupid hearing the words out loud.

Margaret paused. "Are you serious? Now why'd you have to go and ruin this by asking such a silly question?"

Adrian shrugged, shrinking in her chair. "I always got the impression you would have been happier if I hadn't been born."

Margaret sat quietly, and Adrian's chest tightened as she tried not to cry. She felt sheepish for even asking, but she'd always wondered. There was no taking it back now.

"Look at me," Margaret said, and Adrian raised her eyes. "Of course, I was happy to have you. Why would you ever think I wasn't?"

"But I thought you would have preferred pursuing your career and I messed that up..." Adrian said. "You always stressed the importance of that to me."

Margaret swallowed hard. "I'll admit it didn't happen in the timing I'd imagined, but life doesn't always go according to plan. You can attest to that too."

They sat in silence, sipping milk from their mugs. So much to say, and no clue how to say it. "Speaking of, what's going on with the baby?"

"Brian asked Celeste's lawyer to provide documentation of her affair to back up her lien on my house." Adrian felt agitated by the whole situation. She wanted to know Celeste's proof was valid but didn't want to see the proof at all. Seeing the woman's swollen belly was already too much, too painful. She didn't need to see text messages and emails with, "You up?" sent at ten-fifteen pm from her husband, who should have been home with her.

"Christian isn't helping you with this?"

"No, he referred me to his colleague, saying there's a conflict of interest...or was a conflict of interest."

Margaret nodded, and they resumed their silence. Adrian couldn't help feeling like her life was on hold until the baby was born. What was God's plan for her?

"He's an idiot for not calling you, by the way."

"Thanks." Adrian smiled.

They sat together, finishing their milk, truly enjoying each other's company. Before long, they wouldn't be sitting together at the dining table. A sinking feeling washed over Adrian, and she decided she'd cherish the fleeting moments of connectedness with her mother while she still could.

21

_____

Adrian sat across from Brian, clasping her hands into tight fists in her lap. She'd known when he'd asked her to meet with him, he'd probably gotten ahold of Celeste's proof, and she'd reluctantly agreed to meet with him. She'd made some progress in finding a form of peace with Brad's death and infidelity, and yet the Universe kept testing her, keeping her from totally healing.

He pulled a manila file from a stack of folders to his right. "I was able to talk to Celeste's lawyer, and she sent over substantiated evidence of the affair with Brad." His hands fanned over the folder, lifting the corner slightly with a plump finger.

"Is that—?" A lump form in her throat.

"Yes, it is, and you don't have to look at it if you don't want to." His eyes brimmed with sympathy.

Adrian wondered what she would do leading up to that moment, vacillating between looking and not. However, faced with the choice, she knew she needed to see it to make it real, despite her entire body screaming against it. She reluctantly nodded before Brian opened Pandora's Box.

Her eyes scanned the pages, unable to focus on

anything. She saw phone calls and text message history spanning months. Words like *hot, kissing, sexy, tonight*, and *she'll never know* jumped out on the pages, knocking the wind out of Adrian with every blow. But the phrase that pushed her over the edge was, "I love you" from Brad to Celeste on several occasions. That was the knockout.

She quickly closed the folder, bile rising in her throat. "I've seen enough." She pushed it away. Her mind cruelly echoed the three significant words. Every replay dug a hole in her heart, threatening to bleed indigo ink all over the pages of his adultery.

"Adrian, I'm so sorry." His mammoth hand covered hers.

"Please tell me you have good news after that." Her voice trembled.

He sighed. "Well, Celeste has gone missing."

"What do you mean?" How could a pregnant woman just vanish?

"She vacated her apartment and left no forwarding address. Even her lawyer doesn't know where she went."

"So, what now? Could this be seen as a good thing?"

"Unfortunately, it's not that easy." He leaned back in his chair. "We're working on tracking her down, but something tells me she won't stay hidden for long. Not with what's at stake for her."

"Yeah, no kidding." Adrian scoffed.

"Don't worry. We'll find her. I've got a guy I can call for these types of things."

Adrian imagined his guy to be a big mafioso-type, cracking his knuckles and just waiting to be called in. *Sure, I'll find her*, he'd say while cleaning his gun with a microfiber cloth. "Thank you."

After she left his office, she paused in front of Christian's. The door was closed, indicating he was in a meeting. But Adrian didn't care. After seeing Brad's words on the page, she felt annoyed at Christian's silent treatment. She refused to stay in the dark any longer. She needed answers. Immediately.

She opened his office door and their eyes met. He stopped talking, his jaw hanging open.

"Adrian—what?" Christian struggled to form a complete sentence.

He wasn't the only one struggling. Adrian stood in the doorway at a complete loss for words. She felt embarrassed at her rash behavior. "Sorry, I—"

"So, you're Adrian?" Christian's client, a brunette, turned around. She was stunning, with piercing blue eyes and full, pouty lips. She wore a red sundress with a plunging neckline more appropriate for a different kind of meeting as it barely concealed her full bosom. Who was this tramp?

"Sorry, do I know you?"

Christian cleared his throat. "Adrian, this is Sarah."

Realization hit Adrian between the eyes, almost knocking her over. It was his ex, the woman who'd cheated on him. The one who'd broken his heart.

The one he'd planned to propose to.

So, this was why he hadn't called. Sarah was back and clearly seeking Christian's counsel on more than just legal business. A concoction of anger, disappointment, and a touch of heartbreak coursed through her veins. They didn't stand a chance with Sarah back in the picture. It was clear to her now they were over before they'd even started.

"Oh, I get it," she said, finally finding her voice. She looked at Christian, waiting for him to prove her wrong. Waiting for him to say he was helping his ex with any matter not involving the heart. But instead, he looked sheepish, embarrassed for being caught in the act of rekindling things with his ex.

"Adrian, it's—"

"No, no. I get it," She cut him off. She wasn't sure she could handle hearing the truth. She'd seen enough of the truth that day, and her heart couldn't handle any more. She looked at Sarah. "My apologies for interrupting. If you'll excuse me." She closed the door behind her, waiting a moment to see if Christian would come after her. But he didn't. At least now she knew why he hadn't called. She felt proud of herself for restraining her anger, disappointment, and heartache, and for at least making it to her car, where she finally allowed herself to let go, allowing tears to escape.

———

CHRISTIAN FELT SHELL-SHOCKED. Not only was he surprised to see Sarah sitting at his desk waiting for him when he'd returned from a quick errand, but she hadn't had a chance to answer him when he asked why she was there before Adrian walked in.

Of course, he knew it wasn't what it looked like. There wasn't anything going on between him and Sarah, but he didn't have a chance to explain that to Adrian before she'd bolted. Not that he could blame her. If he had walked in and saw her sitting with her ex after not calling, he'd assume the worst too.

"Anyway, where were we?" Sarah said, turning back to face him. "Now that she's gone, there's something I've been wanting to tell you."

"Better make it quick." He had an appointment in the next ten minutes, and even shorter patience for the woman who'd broken his heart.

Sarah flinched, not one to be rushed. "Well, okay then. I'm sure you're wondering why I'm here, and why I emailed you." She waited for him to say something, but he just stared at her. Slightly nervous, she continued. "I'm here because I made a mistake, Christian, and I want you back."

It was what he feared. Part of him was hopeful she reached out in a professional capacity, but he was wrong. He'd turned the possibility over in his mind when he read her initial email, deciding he would only respond when he knew how he would react if she came back saying she'd made a mistake.

On one hand, it was an easy answer. She'd broken his heart. On the day his uncle, who was like a father to him, died. And he'd finally come to peace with it all after months and months of group therapy. He was moving on, or at least trying to, with Adrian.

On the other hand, this was the only woman he'd ever been in love with. They had built a vision of their future together, naming unborn children, even picking out hypothetical nurseries when they were house shopping right before the end. He'd bought a ring. He carried it with him for weeks, waiting for the perfect moment to make it official. He expressed all his hopes and dreams to this woman, and she'd been supportive, encouraging, and everything a true partner should be.

Until she cheated.

"I don't know what you want me to say."

She reached across the desk. "Would it be too much to ask if we could try again?"

Christian sighed as he pulled his hand from hers. "I...I don't know, Sarah." He fixed his eyes on a random spot on his desk.

"Look, I know this isn't what you were expecting, and I've had time to think about it, and you haven't." She leaned down to make eye contact with him. "I'll understand if you need time."

He nodded, looking away from her. Yes, he needed time

to process the conflicting emotions swirling within. He knew if he gave into a second chance they'd fall back into familiarity, re-establishing old routines and habits that fit perfectly like a worn-in shoe. He remembered how her head fit perfectly on his chest, the smell of her hair, how her skin prickled with goose bumps and she tried to resist laughing when he lightly grazed his fingers over her arm while they watched late night shows together in bed. How she took her coffee: Black with stevia. He still had a box of stevia packets in his pantry. How her smile always made him melt, and he'd gotten used to going to sleep listening to her light, rhythmic snoring. It took him months and a white noise machine to break that habit.

Deidre beeped in to notify him his three o'clock was in the lobby waiting for him.

"Would it be too much to ask if you'd like to meet for dinner at the end of this week?"

He paused. Not one to disappoint others, he replied, "Sure."

She smiled, feeling slightly victorious.

"I mean no," he said, finally coming to his senses. "I can't discuss this now, and I don't want to discuss it ever. Sarah, you cheated, end of story. I could never trust you again."

Sarah frowned. "I know this is out of left field, but—"

"But nothing."

Deidre beeped in again.

Sarah didn't move. "So, what? You think that woman... Adrian is right for you?"

He glared at her, feeling his temper flare at her mention of Adrian. "You need to leave."

She stood and smoothed her dress to retain composure. She turned to face him from the doorway, opening her mouth to say something.

"Goodbye, Sarah."

She left without another word.

His heart ached, feeling an old wound threaten to reopen as he forced it to stay closed. To top it all off, he knew Adrian had assumed the worst when she walked into his office. How would he explain to her, someone who knew firsthand what it felt like to be cheated on, that it wasn't what it looked like? Would she even believe him if he tried?

Deidre beeped in again. His heart would have to wait.

22

A drian put the finishing touches on the painting of her mother. It had been a total labor of love, and she'd spent so much time scrutinizing every detail, making sure it was up to snuff. She kept hearing fake criticisms from her mother in her mind every time she thought she'd reached the finish line, making tiny tweaks until she'd reached perfection. Besides, agonizing over the painting had been a welcome distraction from thinking about Christian.

It had been almost a week since she last saw him in his office with Sarah, and she'd allowed herself a day to mope around and consider the possibility of what could have been between them. However, she needed to face reality—it wasn't meant to be. He was obviously rekindling things with his ex. He deserved to be happy. She deserved happiness too, but obviously her happily ever after didn't include him. With everything else going on in her life at the moment, she had too much on her plate to be concerned with a budding relationship anyway. It was definitely all for the best.

She looked the painting over once more, a smile spreading across her lips as she realized she'd done her mother proud. If Margaret didn't agree, she was crazy. It was hands down her best work yet, and her heart burst with excitement from her accomplishment. This was it. This was her destiny, her calling, her reason for being here and nothing, not even a love child, would take it away from her.

She cleaned up her makeshift workstation, carefully carrying her supplies and the painting toward her car. She turned the car over and headed toward her mother's house, dialing Laura on her way back. "Hey, did you know our mothers used to be really close?"

"Good afternoon to you too," Laura said. "And I vaguely remember that. I take it you saw her?"

"Yeah, she found some old photos, one of which was of me and my mom when I was a baby."

"Aw, that's so sweet. Did you show your mom?"

"Yeah, and believe it or not, I think the trip down memory lane did us both some good." Adrian felt a lump form in her throat from thinking about their conversation over the Polaroid. She cleared it. "Anyway, how are you?"

"Good. Dylan is napping, so I'm enjoying the peace and quiet. You know, come to think of it, I remember an argument between our moms about you, I think."

"Why would they argue about me?"

"I don't know. It was a long time ago, but I'm pretty sure my mom mentioned something to your mother about being too hard on you and to stop trying to live her life through you, or something to that effect...I don't really remember."

Adrian considered Laura's words as they tumbled around in her mind. It matched what Elizabeth told her, but she didn't have the faintest memory of any of that happening. She still couldn't help feeling like something was missing from the whole equation. She'd seen her mother be soft with other people in her life, so why had she always been so hard on Adrian in particular?

"Adrian?"

"Sorry, what?"

"Has Brian given you an update on the lien?"

She sighed. "He received the paper trail of Celeste's relationship with Brad, and it was graphic. I couldn't read it all."

"You okay?"

"Peace begins with me, right?" She turned into Shady Acres. The lawn crew was busy manicuring the golf course and trimming bushes. The smell of cut grass permeated her car. "Celeste has gone missing too."

"What do you mean?"

"Apparently, she vacated her apartment and skipped town. No one can find her. But Brian said he knows someone who can."

"Does that mean she's dropping her case?"

"No, it's not that easy, but we'll see what happens once Brian's guy finds her."

"Oh, wait a minute. You haven't mentioned anything about Christian." Her voice was laced with honey. "Did you see him?"

"Oh, yeah. I walked in on him having a meeting with his ex, so that explains why he didn't call. He's getting back together with her."

She paused. "You can't be serious."

"Oh, but I am."

"That doesn't make any sense."

"I know. I don't get it either, but whatever." Adrian feigned nonchalance, but on the inside, her heart sank.

"He's dumber than I thought, and it's obviously his loss," Laura assured her.

"Aw, you always know what to say." Adrian smiled, pulling up to the house. "I better go check on my mom. I told her I'd help get things ready for her friends to come over this evening."

"Is she making pot brownies again?"

Adrian's ears turned red. "After the week I've had, I really hope so."

Laura laughed. "Go have fun. I'll talk to you later."

"Love you."

"Love you more."

———

"ANTE UP," Gilda said, as they gathered around the dining table to play cards after a delicious, green meal. Gilda brought over a chicken curry and Bev brought naan with special herb butter. Margaret and Adrian worked together to make blondies instead of brownies, which looked a little unappetizing with a slightly green tint.

They raised the stakes by playing nickel ante poker instead of gin rummy. Adrian personally had zero poker face, so it was a good thing she brought plenty of nickels. The ladies were likely to clean her out of a whopping three dollars.

Her mother held her cards so close to her chest Adrian wondered if she even knew what she was holding. She admired her mother's courage of staying true to her word, wearing her oxygen even in front of the girls. Bev held her hand a little too loose, revealing she wasn't holding jack squat. Adrian would have expected a loose hold from Gilda, who looked around the table at her competition with a raised eyebrow, sizing them up, preparing to do her worst.

"Hit me," Bev said.

"No, Bev, we're playing Texas Hold 'Em in tribute to Adrian," Margaret said.

"Your bet," Gilda said to Margaret, who raised the stakes a nickel. Everyone checked her bet, and Gilda revealed three cards. Margaret bet three nickels.

"Too hot for me," Bev said, folding her hand. Adrian

agreed with that move based on the woman's hand. At least she knew when to fold 'em.

"Speaking of hot, what's the latest with Christian?" Gilda asked with a sly smile.

"Don't distract me from the high stakes here," Adrian said, dodging the question.

"Has he called?" Bev asked, looking at her with eager eyes.

Adrian matched her mother's bet, attempting to bluff. "No, he hasn't, and I doubt he will." She rested her chin on her hand, covering her mouth as she feigned total concentration on their intense game.

"What makes you say that?" Gilda asked, placing another card in the middle. Adrian sat up a bit straighter now that she had a pair of twos.

"I saw him in his office rekindling things with Sarah, his ex." Adrian shrugged. Margaret raised her bet three more nickels, ruthlessly trying to clean them all out.

"That's absurd," Gilda said, her mouth hanging open. "The hussy that cheated on him?"

"I know, I really don't get it," Adrian said.

"Bev, talk some sense into your nephew," Gilda said, giving her a playful nudge.

Adrian evaluated the current bet and her pair of twos, weighing the options after her mother's heavy-handed bet. "I fold," she said, placing her cards face down. She wished Gilda luck.

"It's too soon for that, isn't it?" Margaret's voice cracked.

"No, I think I'll hang onto my money for the next round."

"Not on the cards, on Christian," Margaret said, taking her eyes off the cards to look at Adrian. The game paused as everyone waited for her response.

"He folded, not me," Adrian said, throwing her hands

up. She watched Gilda place another card in the middle for the final bet.

"That doesn't sound right. I don't see him getting involved with her again. Give him time." Bev touched her hand, giving it a light squeeze. "I'm sure he'll come around."

"Maybe you should show up at his office in fuck me pumps and a trench coat," Gilda said, waiting for Margaret's bet on the last round. "I bet he'll remember to call after that."

Adrian blushed, avoiding eye contact with anyone at the table. Their tryst hadn't exactly involved a trench coat, but...

"Wait, you've already done that haven't you?" Gilda asked, looking at her beet-red face.

"Not exactly," Adrian mumbled.

"You really need to knock some sense into him," Gilda said to Bev.

Bev shrugged. "Maybe he's just scared. He's been through a lot, you know."

"And she hasn't?" Margaret said, surprising Adrian by sticking up for her.

"Alright, enough already. Show me whatcha got," Gilda said. Margaret revealed she only had a pair of twos, and Gilda had three-of-a-kind. She wiggled in her chair in celebration, collecting her winnings by sweeping her arms over the pot.

"You bet it all on a pair of twos?" Adrian asked, dumbfounded. She had the same hand and didn't feel it was worth it.

Margaret nodded. "A pair is always worth betting on."

She was right. All bets were off whenever Adrian was with Christian. She could see herself falling hard for him. But then she remembered he chose someone else. "It takes two to play, though," Adrian said. Gilda shuffled the cards, the sound of fanning and folding as the two halves merged back into one deck echoed in the room. "Hey, isn't it time for a brownie or whatever the hell we made?"

"You sure you can hang?" Margaret raised an eyebrow.

"Without a doubt." Adrian slapped the table and went to get the blondies. "I'm your daughter, right?" She grinned, slicing into the pan.

"Absolutely." Margaret beamed. Gilda passed out the cards, and they placed starting bets again. Adrian bit into a blondie, the rich buttery taste tickling her tongue.

"He'll ante up again, you know," Bev assured her. Adrian felt skeptical but hopeful that she was right.

———

ADRIAN PUT the last glass in the dishwasher before starting it, then wiped down the table to help clean up after the poker game. Margaret put the cards away in her room and went to get ready for bed.

As Adrian looked around to see if anything still needed picking up, she couldn't help thinking about the poker game and her mother's words of wisdom: *A pair is always worth betting on.* Was she really ready to place her bets again? Unfortunately, the one man she wanted had folded before the game really started. But if anything, her experience with Christian assured her she could, and would, move on from Brad.

It warmed her heart thinking about her mother sticking up for her with Bev. She couldn't recall another time when that had happened. And yes, Bev was right. Adrian knew Christian had been through a lot, but honestly, at their age, who hadn't? Everyone has a story to tell, but she knew with absolute certainty the story she'd yet to tell would be more interesting than her old one. She wanted to keep the old in her rear-view, focusing on what she could see in the headlights traveling down the new road to her future. Time would tell who would join her on the new journey.

A knock at the door interrupted her thoughts. Maybe one of the girls forgot something. A big bouquet of stargazer lilies and roses greeted her with their heady fragrance as she opened the door, Harold hidden behind them. He'd combed his hair, using pomade to make it stay in place, and had on a gray sportcoat and a buttercream buttoned shirt. A hint of Old Spice mixed with the flowers.

"Margaret—" he started, stopping when he saw Adrian. "Oh, where's your mother?" His cheeks turned pink. The last time they'd seen each other, Harold was in Margaret's bathrobe. At least this time he was fully clothed.

"I'll go get her."

"I'm right here," she said. Her eyes sparkled when she saw Harold and the flowers.

"Margaret, I've been thinking." He walked toward her, carefully balancing the bouquet in his shaky hand. "I know we probably don't have much time left, but I can't imagine spending another moment without you. I love you, and I'll love you as long as I live." His voice cracked at the end, tears forming in the corners of his eyes.

Margaret, who normally displayed little emotion, had tears pooling in her eyes too. Her complexion dewy and glowing, she beamed with excitement. "Oh, Harold," she crooned. He handed the flowers to Adrian and let them go, wrapping both arms around Margaret's frail body. They held each other, both of their cheeks wet with tears, getting lost in each other's embrace. Adrian retreated to the kitchen to put the flowers in a vase, leaving them to their privacy.

She could hear them mumbling sweetly to one another and giggling like teenagers. The smacking of their kisses echoed off the thin walls as Adrian trimmed the flowers and arranged them in a crystal vase. It warmed her heart to see her mother so happy. She deserved it, and Adrian admired her courage for taking a leap with her heart. And yes, Harold was right. There wasn't much time left for them to share, but they were determined to make the most of it. How easy they both made it look.

Well, was it really that hard?

With Christian, things felt just as easy, which made it even harder to believe he was giving up on them, returning to his ex. Regardless, Adrian knew she was worth betting on. Eventually, she'd find someone who would place their bets on her and not fold early.

Her mother and Harold retreated to the bedroom, closing the door behind them. Adrian turned out all the lights and headed to bed, thankful that her room was on the opposite side of the house. If that failed, there were always earplugs.

23

The day started out like any ordinary day, although the events that would unfold made it a day Adrian would never forget.

Adrian started the day painting at the beach. Painting left her with a feeling of fulfillment like nothing else had. She was finally taking the steps to create the life she'd always dreamed of, and she wished her dad was there to see her. She had a feeling he was cheering her on from somewhere in the ethers.

That day, she would give her mother the painting she'd done of her. She couldn't wait to give it to her, showing her how far she'd come as an artist and that it was more than a hobby. She wanted her mother to see herself as she saw her, hoping to eliminate any fear Margaret might be feeling with her time coming to an end.

When she arrived home, no talking heads greeted her, the house eerily quiet. Her mother wasn't in her usual chair in the living room, and the bedroom door was ajar, with darkness beyond the frame. Adrian quickly retrieved the painting from her bedroom closet, placing her supplies at the foot of the bed before heading toward her mother's room.

She peered in to see if her mother was awake. She lay motionless, except for the shallow rising and falling of her chest, indicating she was still breathing. Adrian heard the gentle whirring of her oxygen machine in the background. Her eyes were closed, and Adrian decided to let her rest.

"Boo," Margaret said with a smile. She opened her eyes and saw the painting in Adrian's hands. "Is that for me?"

"Yes, but I can show you later. You should rest."

"No need." She struggled to sit up, and Adrian set the painting down to help. Margaret thanked her, and Adrian realized how much her mother had softened in the last few months. "Now will you show me?"

"Before I do that, I want to share a story with you." Adrian cleared a lump in her throat. "After my accident, I went to Heaven. A beautiful little girl greeted me and told me I couldn't stay, as much as I wanted to. Heaven is so real, and it's amazing." She grabbed her mother's bony hand. "There's nothing but love that exists there, and to be honest, it was so hard to leave. But the little girl told me I had more to do here." She choked up, taking a deep breath before finishing. "She told me you needed my help," she continued, her voice shaky. "And I'm so glad I listened to her." She brushed away tears. Her mother's eyes were damp as she attempted to squeeze Adrian's hand. "I know things haven't always been easy between us, but I've enjoyed the last few months. I feel like I finally have my mom back." She reluctantly let her mother's hand go to pick up the painting. "I wanted you to have this." She revealed the painting of her mother and the little girl holding hands together, walking in a golden field toward the bright light of Heaven.

"You made this?" Margaret asked, and Adrian nodded. She studied the painting in awe. "It's remarkable."

It was the first time Margaret had paid Adrian a true compliment on anything she'd done artistically, and it warmed her heart in a way she'd never felt before. She'd grown accustomed to never receiving acceptance on any of her choices, but to finally have it released a weight of inadequacy she'd been carrying around her whole life.

"This is how I see you." She held the painting in her lap. "I know she'll be there to greet you like she did me, and you'll experience the overwhelming waves of love from God wash over you."

"How can you be so sure?" Margaret furrowed her brow. "I haven't been all that good." Before Adrian could say anything to the contrary, she held up her hand. "I need to say something." Margaret breathed deeply, appearing to search for the right words and courage to say what needed to be said years ago. "I never should have discouraged your artistic side. You're very talented, and I always knew that." Her voice cracked. "I'm ashamed to admit it, but I was jealous of how close you were to your father. I wanted you to take after me, and I am so sorry." Tears streamed down ravines in her face.

Adrian replayed her mother's words in her mind, the validity of words she'd longed to hear sinking in. She stared in disbelief, seeing her emotions flooding her mother's face. The need for parental approval never disappears, and her mother had validated Adrian's talent. She felt compassion as she looked into Margaret's regretful eyes.

"You did the best you could." For the first time in her life, she truly believed that. Despite her mother's flaws, she knew deep down she meant well. And there she was, in her final moments, feeling scared and alone. Adrian wanted nothing more than to take that fear away. "There's nothing to fear, Ma. Where you're going is so much better than anything down here."

"Even Harold?" Margaret smiled weakly.

Adrian chuckled. "Yes, even Harold doesn't hold a candle."

Margaret considered her words. "I hope you're right."

Adrian saw her mother struggling to breathe, but sadly, her own body was the enemy as she drowned from the inside out.

"You have too, you know," Margaret said.

"What's that?" Adrian brushed hair back from her mother's forehead. Tiny beads of sweat pooled near her hairline.

"Done your best," she said. "I know I didn't approve of Brad, and for good reason, but I'm proud of you for standing by him, even though I lost you for a little while."

"Really?" Adrian felt dumbfounded. Her mother had never told her she was proud of her. Why had they waited so long to be honest?

"Yes, and I'm sorry I haven't said anything until now. But I need you to do something for me."

"Anything." Adrian wiped a tear from her chin.

"Make up with Christian," she said. "I want you to experience love like I had with George, and I've found again with Harold. I've seen the way he looks at you. What you two have...that doesn't come along every day."

She certainly had tall orders, considering Christian's ex was back in the picture. "I'll try."

Margaret wrapped a frail arm around her neck, pulling her into a hug. Adrian could feel her mother's frailty as she held her in her arms, both of their bodies shaking with emotion.

"Will you get me some water?" Margaret asked. Adrian reluctantly let her go before fulfilling her mother's request. She'd never seen her mother so weak, so vulnerable. Adrian took a deep breath and wiped her tear-stained cheeks. She needed to be strong to help balance and ground her mother.

That's what she'd do if roles were reversed. She put on a brave face and headed back to Margaret's room with water glass in hand.

When she returned, the energy had shifted. The room felt empty, cold, and lifeless. Adrian feared the worst as the hair stood up on the back of her neck. Frozen in place, she gripped the glass of water so hard her hand started to cramp. "Ma?" Her throat constricted. The gentle hum of the oxygen machine was the only reply.

Adrian approached her mother's lifeless body. Margaret looked peaceful, staring at the painting Adrian had just given her. Adrian waited for her mother to blink but knew that wouldn't happen. She dropped to her knees, her body convulsing as she grabbed her mother's hand and held it to her face. She imagined the little girl reaching for that hand as they lay in the field of daffodils, naming what shapes they saw in the perfectly puffy clouds.

Adrian gently closed her mother's eyelids and made a cross over her chest with her hands. She looked like she was just napping, but this time, she wouldn't wake up. Adrian was an orphan, a stray weaned too soon. She leaned down and hugged her mother's lifeless body as she wept, her tears staining the shoulder of Margaret's light pink nightgown. "I love you, Ma." She kissed her forehead.

Adrian had known this day would come, but it didn't make the stark reality of her mother's departure any easier. There were still so many things left unsaid, and they would forever remain so. Desperate to hear a friendly voice, she wiped the tears from her face and dialed the familiar number.

"Finally," Laura said when she answered. When Adrian couldn't find the words to respond, she said, "Is this a butt dial?"

"No," Adrian blurted. "She's gone."

"Oh, honey. I'm so sorry." Her voice was full of compassion. "Are you okay? What happened?"

Adrian tried to tell her, but nothing would come out except tears. Laura was patient while she cried. "We were talking, and I went to get her a glass of water and then..." Adrian trailed off, unable to finish, afraid finishing the sentence would make it more real and final. Could it all possibly be a dream?

"Say no more. I'll be there as soon as I can."

24

The next few days were a blur. Laura arrived two days later and helped Adrian plan the service for Margaret. She was so thankful to have another body in the house. It was eerily quiet without the whirring of her mother's oxygen machine or the incessant news blaring through the TV. She tried her best to compartmentalize her thoughts and feelings, knowing there was much to be done in her mother's honor. But she would often stare off into space, Laura touching her hand to bring her back to the present, asking for input on various plans. Adrian would nod and go along with whatever Laura was saying, lacking the energy for anything beyond that.

Bev and Gilda were a huge help, assisting in making arrangements. Margaret had shared her ideas with them about what kind of service she preferred. In all the time Adrian had spent with her, she'd never thought to ask. In hindsight, it seemed silly to avoid talking about the inevitable, but she was glad her mother shared her wishes with someone.

Margaret wanted to be cremated, not buried, and wanted her ashes scattered in the Gulf. She also wished for a celebration of life instead of a traditional vigil. Given her traditional Catholic upbringing, those plans surprised Adrian. Even in death, her mother was full of surprises. Gilda told her she'd only recently changed her wishes, saying Adrian had influenced her decision. Margaret had trusted her daughter to make the right plans for the memorial, and Adrian felt honored she'd trusted her that much. Perhaps, in her own way, this was Margaret showing Adrian she loved her. It only took her dying to express it.

They decided to hold a memorial service at the Orange Blossom Rec Center so others in the neighborhood who knew her could easily attend. Laura and Adrian looked through old photo albums to find the right images that summed up Margaret's life, including the one Laura's mom gave to her. Bev provided a few recent ones, including one of Margaret and Adrian from a recent poker night. Adrian stood behind her mother, Margaret resting her hand on her daughter's forearm, both of them smiling. Seeing the light in her mother's eyes made Adrian choke up. She'd give anything to hug her mother again. It was too soon for her to be gone.

They set up in the back part of the main atrium, with a table filled with snacks and sandwiches for anyone who had an appetite. The high ceilings and opaque natural lighting cast the perfect glow over the somber group. Adrian didn't have a chance to get a new dress for the occasion, but fortunately had a black maxi dress that would have to do. The turnout for her mother's celebration surprised her. There were many faces she'd never seen before, the room buzzing with memories of Margaret. Laura's parents were there, and Elizabeth pulled Adrian in for a wordless hug. She cradled Adrian's head in her hand like a mother would, and Adrian didn't want to break the connection.

"I am so sorry, Adrian," Elizabeth said, her eyes damp. "I

really wish things had turned out differently for all of us." Adrian could see Elizabeth's mind reeling over not making peace with Margaret before she died.

"Thank you." Adrian took a deep breath, trying her best to hold it together. She needed to be strong, to make her mother proud. "I told Ma about my visit with you, and she didn't say much, but I could tell from the look in her eye she missed you too." Elizabeth shed a tear at her words. "I don't mean to upset you or make you feel guilty. I just thought I'd tell you that, hoping it helps. You know my mom...a woman of few words." Adrian forced a smile.

Elizabeth nodded. "Thank you." She hugged Adrian, and this time, Adrian cradled her perfect French twist in her hand.

"Think you're up for saying a few words?" Laura asked. Adrian nodded, and parted from Elizabeth.

She clinked a plastic knife against a red solo cup, which didn't do much to draw attention. Gilda whistled like she was hailing a cab in New York to bring attention to Adrian. She felt nervous with all eyes on her, waiting for something profound to come out of her mouth.

"Thank you all so much for coming. As many of you know, Margaret was my mother." *She's still my mother. Death doesn't change that, right?* "She was tough as nails on me growing up, and I'm sure that's no surprise to those who knew her." A few chuckles peppered the room. "And while we didn't always see eye to eye, as it was always her way or no way..." Adrian trailed off. This wasn't a time to go there, and she felt the room tense up. She looked at the photograph of her mother smiling at her as a baby. "I've spent the last five months taking care of my mother, and I've learned she's full of surprises." She smiled thinly at Bev and Gilda. "I'm so grateful for the time I spent with her, and if I can be just half as brave, resilient, and strong as she was, I'll count myself lucky." She saw lots of heads nod throughout the crowd and searched for more to say. Whatever was left would remain unsaid, as her emotions overtook her. "Thank you."

Laura came to Adrian's side, looking perfect in her black shift dress. "Would anyone else like to share a few words about Margaret?" she asked the group while gently rubbing Adrian's back.

Many people took turns sharing stories about Margaret. Adrian couldn't recall the detail, only the emotion behind the stories left an impression. She appreciated everyone who spoke and had no idea what an impact her mother had on the small community. Once everyone went back to idle chit chat, Adrian saw Harold across the room, standing alone by the table showcasing the photos. He seemed completely lost without her mother, and her heart ached for him. She placed a hand on his shoulder.

"I'd ask if you're okay, but...I think I already know the answer."

He turned and hugged her, catching her off-guard. "I can't believe she's already gone." His voice cracked from holding back tears. "Sorry." He pulled away, brushing himself off.

"Have you eaten anything?" She already knew and didn't wait for his response. "Come on, let's get some food." She linked her arm in his to lead him toward the spread. After much coercing, he finally grabbed a small plate of food, which she suspected was only to appease her. Her heart hurt even more to see his breaking.

Every time a new face walked into the room, she'd secretly hoped to see Christian. But as the crowd began to thin, she realized he wasn't going to show. Maybe it was time for her to grieve the loss of what could have been there too.

Bev, Gilda, Laura and Adrian cleaned up the space. The

others put Adrian in charge of collecting the photographs, and she studied each one before stacking them for transport. She grabbed the guest book, vowing to read the comments later. She was too raw to face it right then.

"Okay, I think that's the last of it." Laura examined the room for anything out of place. "You ready?"

Adrian nodded. It was time to move on in many ways.

THE DAY after Margaret's celebration, Laura stayed to help Adrian sort through her mother's belongings. No one talks about all the work that comes along with a loved ones' death. The death is just the beginning. It was a cruel joke, sifting through all the things that surrounded her mother in life, seeing the lifelessness without her touch. What would her mother want her to do with all of her treasures? If only she could ask.

They tackled the bedroom first, dividing items into donate and keep piles. The experience was anything but glamorous, seeing stacks of half-empty pill bottles and disposing of Margaret's old toothbrush, the bristles spread out from overuse. But somehow, being around her stuff made Adrian feel close to her again. She could see her mother in her mind's eye, perched on the corner of her bed, reminding them to be careful with her things. Adrian smiled at the thought.

She cleaned out the bedside table, which held a copy of the Bible, worn with age. She found a collection of old cards from birthdays and anniversaries over the years, including a yellowed page with crude crayon drawings of a woman and child holding hands under a fragmented rainbow. She instantly recognized her ancient penmanship: *I love you mommy* scribbled in pink and red. Her mother had kept it all those years? Adrian teared up, thinking about her mother holding a different little girl's hand now.

She opened the jewelry box on the top of her mother's dresser to sort through her treasures. There were several gifts from her father, including a solitaire diamond necklace he gave her for their twenty-fifth anniversary. Adrian saw her parents' wedding bands next to each other, both tarnished with age and neglect. Definitely going in the keep pile. She held them tightly in her hand and thought about melting them down. Maybe she could make something new with the symbols of their love for one another. Something she could carry with her, always keeping them close.

"So, what now?" Laura asked, folding Margaret's favorite blue dress to put in the donate pile.

"What do you mean?"

"What's next for you?" Laura pulled more clothes off hangers, including the black and white shirt her mother wore to their last poker game. "You don't have your mom to look after anymore. Think you'll come back to Austin?"

Adrian paused. "I don't know yet." She hadn't given any thought to herself, the bulk of her attention on her mother as of late.

"I'm sure you could find another tech job pretty easily if you wanted to."

Adrian pulled clothing from her mother's dresser. "That definitely doesn't interest me."

"Well, you still have a home there. We could pull it off the market."

"No, I don't want to live in the house with Brad's memory. I need a fresh start, new energy."

"You're starting to sound like me." Laura smiled. "And I agree, although selfishly I want you to come back to Austin."

"I know, and I haven't ruled anything out yet." She hadn't received an offer on the house yet because of Celeste's lien, and Laura told her she'd have to disclose that to potential buyers. It would take the right buyer to come along and be patient while they worked things out, and those people were on par with unicorns.

Laura's phone rang. From her body language, Adrian knew it was Zach. She heard her friend coo at Dylan, and her tone changed when Zach was back on the line. "No, I don't know." Laura placed a hand on her hip. "As long as she needs me." She paced a little. "Yes, I know. Call you later, okay? Love you." She hung up.

"Do you need to get back?" Adrian asked when Laura returned. She felt selfish and greedy, keeping her best friend hostage when her family needed her.

"No, not at all. I'm here as long as you need me. It's fine."

They resumed sorting through Margaret's stuff.

"Do you miss them?"

"Of course," Laura said, folding a purple floral dress Adrian had never seen. "Although, if I'm honest, it's been nice and quiet without a crying baby around." She looked surprised at her own honesty. "Am I a terrible mom for saying that?"

Adrian realized in her best friend's question indicated how much women judge one another, holding each other to impossibly high standards and criticizing others behind their backs when they didn't follow suit in what they *should* do according to the female collective. Women spend so much time tearing each other down and should redirect that energy into lifting each other up. Her mother had always been concerned about other people's opinions to the point she wouldn't even wear her oxygen in public. And there Adrian was, afraid to live her life the way she wanted to out of fear of what other people might think. *Has Brad been buried long enough for me to move on? Should I go back to the safety of a soulless corporate job?* The apple didn't fall far, did it?

Adrian looked at her best friend, seeing her as a woman first and not just a mom. Just because she had a baby didn't mean she stopped being who she was pre-baby. And there was no reason a baby should completely change a person. Obviously, there would be a priority shift, but Laura was still a priority too.

Adrian thought about her mother, realizing she was a woman first too and not just her mother. She was certain there were times Margaret desperately wanted to get away and fuel her own interests and passions but couldn't. It gave Adrian a newfound respect for both of them. "No." She smiled. "And thank you."

"For what?" Laura pushed a curl behind her ear.

"Your motherly and womanly wisdom."

Laura furrowed her brow, and her phone rang again. She rolled her eyes and answered it. That time, Adrian knew it was business, and she sifted through more of her mother's possessions.

"I just received a verbal offer on your house."

Adrian's jaw dropped. "How much?"

"Full price." Laura forced a smile.

A sense of relief washed over her. "That solves one problem."

"What's that?"

"Where I'm going to live." She fidgeted with a pair of holey socks. "I guess there's no turning back now."

"You know you always have a home in Austin with me if you want to come back."

She thought about Karen and Susan and everyone else in her group. She also thought about Bev and Gilda and poor lost Harold. "I think I might stick around here for a while. I don't know how to explain it, but I feel like there's more to do. Other people who need me."

"To say I'm surprised would be an understatement." Laura struggled to hide her disappointment. "You sure you won't change your mind and come back?"

"Somehow, this feels like where I need to be. At least, for now."

Laura nodded in acceptance, and they resumed packaging up Margaret's belongings, going through the items that were a small reflection of the woman she was.

25

Laura had a few errands to run, which gave Adrian an opportunity to paint. She couldn't find the right subject for her next painting, assuming inspiration would hit once she settled into her usual spot near the beach. She kept thinking about her mother. What would she be doing now? She smiled at the thought of her finding something in Heaven to criticize. Perhaps her tired mind was finally able to rest.

Adrian's heart ached. Part of her wished her mother were still there. She'd give anything to hear her nag her again. The other part of her knew she'd finally found peace and no longer felt pain. She was able to breathe easily with her Heavenly lungs, free from a body attacking itself and drowning in accumulated phlegm. The idea made it easier to cope.

Adrian held a pencil, ready to sketch an idea. She contemplated how the blankness of the paper reflected her mind. She felt drained from the last week of saying goodbye and the aftermath of her mother's passing. Fortunately, group would start soon, and she felt relieved to have the support to lean on.

Resolved with a few random doodles, she cleared her space and made her way to the familiar pavilion early. Karen was the first one there, putting out folding chairs. Adrian rushed over to help.

"Thank you," she said. Karen looked at her and knew before Adrian could confess. "Oh dear. I'm so sorry." She placed a warm hand on Adrian's shoulder, pulling her into a hug. "How are you holding up, kiddo?"

Adrian shed a tear. "I'm okay. One day at a time, right?"

Karen looked at her with deeply empathetic eyes. "I would have thought you'd be hightailing it back to Austin now that your mom is gone."

"I thought about that, but I'm not sure I'm ready to leave yet. I don't know how to explain it, but I still feel there's more to do here." She realized in that moment how much she'd changed since her accident. In the past, she never put much stock into gut feelings, but now, she allowed her intuition to guide her, and it was shouting for her to stay.

"You're always welcome here, you know," Karen said. "You're definitely part of the group."

As Adrian looked at Karen, she thought about Gilda and Bev. And poor lost Harold. They'd become a little family to her in the last few months, and she couldn't bear the thought of leaving them. It was almost like they still harbored a piece of her mother, whom she longed to be close to in every way possible. "Yeah, I think you're stuck with me." She shrugged.

"I'm glad."

Her phone buzzed. Brian's name popped up on the caller ID, and she excused herself from Karen to answer.

"We finally tracked her down." Adrian felt relieved at his words. "She's in labor."

"Labor? Where?"

"In a hospital in Lubbock. I'll let you know more as I find out, but I at least wanted to let you know we found her."

"Thanks, Brian. Keep me posted." She hung up, turning back to Karen. "I'm so sorry, I can't stay—"

"Go on. It's okay. We'll catch up next week. We're here for you," Karen assured.

"Thank you." Adrian headed toward her car, desperate to talk to Laura. Soon enough, there would be resolution one way or the other on whether Brad had fathered Celeste's baby. The outcome didn't change the fact that he cheated but finding out the results of the paternity test was the last piece of the puzzle, and for better or worse, Celeste was about to complete it.

———

CHRISTIAN PULLED into the parking lot for group just in time to see Adrian drive away. He hoped he hadn't been the cause for her early departure, and his heart sank. He'd picked up his phone several times, ready to dial her number, but his mind would overthink what to say, paralyzing him from action. He thought he'd figure out what to say when he saw her in person. Even if the words weren't right, at least they'd be talking. But she'd just left.

He made his way over to group, early for once. Frank assisted Karen by putting out carafes of coffee and water, and Henry hummed while he formed a circle with folding chairs. Christian could tell Karen was reassuring Gina about something. Had she lost weight since he'd seen her last? Susan even appeared to be more tolerant than usual, a smile replacing her normal scowl as she smoked a cigarette.

"Christian, so glad you could make it," Karen said, giving him a quick hug.

"Where's Adrian?" He asked.

"Oh, she had to go. Something about labor. I'm not sure."

Christian knew immediately what happened. Celeste must have gone into labor. He'd call Brian later to get an update.

"Since he's early for once, should we go ahead and get started?" Frank teased.

"Ha-ha," Christian said, playfully pushing Frank's arm.

Karen shrugged. "We might as well, since Adrian won't be here today. Oh, and the next time you see her, please be kind. She just lost her mother."

Sounds of empathy echoed throughout the group, and Christian's stomach dropped. Unscripted or not, he needed to call her later. There were still a few things that left him feeling uncertain but being there for Adrian during a time of need wasn't one of them.

"Which is a nice segue," Karen continued, "into our topic this week, which is moving on with our lives. Sometimes it can feel overwhelming thinking about moving on without your loved one, especially when you go back to your normal routine, realizing that person is no longer a part of it. However, you're still here, and it's important to establish a new routine or try new things and create healthy habits for yourself."

Christian chuckled under his breath. Had Karen developed the ability to read minds?

"Christian, did you have something to add?" she asked.

"Actually, I was thinking how appropriate this topic is for me this week."

"Care to elaborate?"

"Sure." He sat up a little straighter. "My ex, the one who cheated on me, recently showed up to my office asking for a second chance. It was the last thing I expected, and I actually considered it. I'd be lying if I said I wasn't disappointed in myself for wanting to slide back into the familiar."

"Don't beat yourself up," Frank said. "We all know how hard that break-up was for you. I'd be surprised if you hadn't considered it, even for a minute."

"Well, to make matters worse, I'd recently started seeing someone, and she happened to walk into my office while Sarah was there. She didn't give me a chance to explain, but I was at a loss for words at the time anyway."

"Is it Adrian?" Henry asked, surprising Christian. "I've seen the way you look at her. It reminds me of how I looked at Betty, the most gorgeous woman on the planet." He had a dreamy look in his eyes.

"Well, since you already know, yeah, it is. Or was." He shifted uncomfortably. "I'm afraid my past is getting in the way of my future, whatever that might look like at this point."

"Have you talked to her since?" Gina asked.

"No, I was hoping to get a chance to today, but she left before I could."

"Just to be clear, you said no to your ex, right?" Susan asked.

"Yes, but to be honest, the whole situation made me wonder if I'm ready to move on."

"It's okay to take time to figure it out," Karen said. "You don't need to know all the answers right now."

"But a woman like Adrian doesn't come along every day," Gina said. "Just look at how much she's impacted all of our lives in the time she's been here. You'd be crazy to let her go."

"Don't add pressure to the man," Susan admonished. "If it's meant to be, it'll work out."

"Although it'd be awkward for us if you don't work it out." Frank grimaced.

"Just listen to your heart. It won't steer you wrong," Karen said.

Christian considered Karen's words. Was he going to continue playing it safe, or would he go after what he knew would bring him true happiness? When he pictured moving forward with the rest of his life, there was one piece missing. One woman who completed the puzzle. He'd suspected it for years but now knew with complete certainty he had to at least try. If he struck out, at least he'd go out swinging.

"It looks like you figured out what to do, am I right?" Henry asked.

Christian nodded.

"Good. Go get our girl," Gina said.

"Oh, for crying out loud, Gina." Susan rolled her eyes.

They laughed as Christian devised his plan for moving on with his life.

———

ADRIAN HAD BEEN LOOKING FORWARD to group therapy all week, but after Brian called, there was no way she would have been present enough to honor everyone there. She'd wondered if Christian would show and had rehearsed aloof responses if he tried addressing the elephant named Sarah in the room. She needed to obsess for one last time on the potential outcome with her best friend. She felt relieved to see Laura's car parked along the curb outside her mother's house as she pulled into the driveway.

"I have so much to tell you," they both said simultaneously when Adrian walked through the door. After much debate about who should go first, Laura let Adrian have the floor.

"Celeste is in labor." She shared the details from her short conversation with Brian.

"Wow, I guess we'll know soon enough once and for all, huh?" Laura sat on the sofa, looking perfectly put together in black yoga pants and a short-sleeved pink t-shirt. Her hair balanced on top of her head in a messy bun, a couple of loose tendrils framing her face.

Adrian settled into her mother's chair. "Brian promised to call me the moment he finds out." She pulled her phone out of her pocket and set it on the armrest, directly in view. "I'll just be glad to have some finality one way or another. The limbo has been painful." Laura nodded her head in agreement. "Okay, what were you going to tell me?"

"You won't believe who I ran into while I was out. Do you remember Denise Perkins?" she asked. Adrian wrinkled her forehead, coming up short after searching her memory. "Denise was a year ahead of us in school...she's now Denise Buchanan. Anyway, she's opening an art gallery in Pensacola, and when I told her about you, she wanted to see your work." Laura struggled to sit still, beaming with excitement.

"Seriously?" Adrian couldn't believe it. Was it the sign she'd been looking for? Was she finally in the right place at the right time, doing the right thing? Her heart soared at the Universe's orchestration.

"Yeah, she said she'd love to support a fellow Pirate alumnus."

"Once a Pirate, always a Pirate, right?" Adrian smiled, not even remotely nauseous at saying something so trite. She couldn't wait to get away from high school, and now she reclaimed her alliance with fervor.

"I guess you will be sticking around here for a while after all." Laura picked a piece of imaginary lint from her shirt.

"It seems like things are lining up for me that way." They sat in silence for a moment, the reality of living in separate towns more permanently hanging heavy in the air. Adrian recognized the war raging inside of her best friend instantly, for the same war raged within her. On one hand, she was excited, but on the other, it meant they'd be apart. Neither one of them were ever good with that, always finding a way to stick together. But it seemed this time they might be forced to stay apart. Adrian needed to figure out a way to convince her and Zach to move back to Florida.

"I wonder who Celeste will list as the father on the birth certificate," she said.

Before Adrian could answer, there was a knock at the door. It was Gilda and Bev, who had on velour tracksuits, and Bev held tiny weights in both hands. Gilda's sweatband pushed her hair straight up like a cockatoo's.

"As much as we'd like to, we're not going to stay long," Bev said, adjusting her blue knitted hat.

At Adrian's look of confusion, Gilda held out an envelope. "Margaret left this with us for you."

Adrian's pulse raced as she took the envelope. Her name was scrawled in her mother's shaky penmanship across the front. She wasn't sure what to say or if she had the strength to open it.

"We'll be by later to check on you," Gilda said, touching her shoulder before shutting the door gently.

"I think I need to check in with Zach," Laura said before Adrian could say anything. She stepped away, leaving Adrian alone with a letter from her mother. She sat in her mother's chair and opened it, bracing for Margaret's last words to her.

DEAR ADRIAN,

I know you always believed I didn't want children. Having a baby was a shock to me, and I wasn't sure I could handle the responsibility and what it takes to raise a child. To be honest, I was afraid to have a girl who would be just like me. But God has a funny sense of humor sometimes, and of course, He blessed me with you. You're just like me in many ways, but you took after the best parts of your father too.

You may believe I was too hard on you. One thing I never got a chance to tell you is I suffered from what doctors now call post-partum depression. In the spirit of honesty, I felt guilty for my depression when you were a baby, and perhaps I was too critical at times. It's only because I had great expectations for you and always wanted the best. There was so much I missed out on, too many roads not taken, and I didn't want you to follow in my foot-steps. In hindsight, I wouldn't change a thing about my life, especially you.

I'm sorry there was a period of time in our lives when we didn't speak, and I regret missing out on your life, from the big events to the mundane. I'm even more sorry it took my getting sick to bring us back together. But if I had to die for us to find our way back to each other, I was glad to do it, and I'd do it again a thousand times.

I want to thank you for the love and kindness you've shown me over the last few months, even though, at times, I felt I didn't deserve it. You are a remarkable woman, and I am so proud of you. Don't ever settle. Life is fragile, and it can be taken away in an instant, and it's always over far more quickly than you'd like.

I love you, always.
Mom

ADRIAN SOBBED as she read it again twice. She wiped her tears away, sniffling from a runny nose. Her chest felt tight, squeezing her heart as it broke into a million pieces. Laura crouched next to her and, without a word, wrapped her arm around Adrian, pulling her into a hug as she broke down.

Laura rubbed Adrian's back as she convulsed, letting emotions out she'd harbored for too long.

Her mother was proud of her. She loved her. She'd longed to hear those words her entire life, and there they were, commemorated in her letter. *Don't ever settle, life is fragile.* Her mother's words replayed in her mind. For the first time in her life, Adrian vowed to honor her mother's wishes.

26

———

"You sure you'll be okay?" Laura asked, slamming her trunk shut. Adrian's heart sank. She'd known the day would come the moment she'd arrived, but she wasn't ready for Laura to leave. She had no idea how long it would be before they saw each other again, with life leading them in separate directions.

"Yes, I'll be fine," Adrian reassured, trying to convince herself too. "You need to get home to your family."

Laura shielded her eyes from the mid-morning sun, already burning bright. "What's next for Adrian?"

"I don't know. I think I'll call Denise and see if she wants to have lunch this week." She smiled.

"That's a great idea." She stood there, stalling, obviously not wanting to leave. Someone had to rip off the Band-Aid.

"Call me as soon as you get home." Adrian hugged her tightly. "Thank you again for everything. I don't know what I'd do without you."

"That's what friends are for." Laura smiled.

They said their goodbyes and Laura drove away. Adrian waved to her until she was out of view. She went back inside to finish the last of her coffee in her mother's chair. The house was so quiet, no oxygen or news blaring in the background. Just her, Joe, and her mind's endless chatter. It was the first time she'd been alone with her thoughts in days. *Where do I go from here?*

A knock interrupted her thoughts. Was Laura back already? She jumped to open the door. "Did you forget something?" But it wasn't Laura who greeted her.

It was Christian.

"Oh...what are you doing here?" Her nerves kicked into high gear seeing him. He looked impeccably put together as always, wearing a gray pinstripe suit and a violet tie. She pulled her bathrobe a little tighter, feeling severely under-dressed for this unexpected house call. She steadied herself against the doorframe, her knees weakened from the faint smell of his aftershave.

"Brian was tied up this morning, so I told him I'd deliver the news to you about the baby." Adrian stood at the door, waiting for him to say more, but he didn't. "Do you mind if I...?"

"Sorry." She moved out of the way as he walked over the threshold. She felt queasy, her body surging with caffeine and adrenaline. He shut the door behind him, and they stood there awkwardly for a moment. Damn, he looked good. But seeing him felt premature, and she had too many open wounds to deal with the possibility of another. "Do you want coffee?" she asked, filling the void.

"No, let's just sit down." They walked toward the living room, a sense of dread washing over her. It must be bad. A house call and not cutting to the chase? She felt faint.

She turned around, steadying herself on his arm. "Just tell me. Is the baby Brad's?"

"Doubtful."

"What do you mean?"

"Brad wasn't black, was he?" She shook her head. "Well, the baby has dark skin, taking after whomever the father is."

"Seriously?" He nodded. She couldn't help but laugh with relief, cackling a bit like a hyena. "But she was so sure it was Brad's."

"Apparently, Celeste conveniently forgot about a one-night stand." He smirked.

"That's very convenient"

He shrugged. "Yep, I'm pleased to say you're off the hook. She's dropped everything."

Adrian couldn't believe it. She'd dodged a serious bullet, the Universe seamlessly tying up her loose ends. She could finally move forward with her future plans, making the next phase of her life whatever she wanted without interference from anyone else. The house was under contract, and now there wasn't a lien or a baby standing in the way.

"Wow, thank you." She went to hug him in all the excitement, but stopped short, her arms flailing nervously like she was directing aircraft. "Um...is that all?" She ran a hand through her hair and looked down at the ground, trying her best to play it all off.

"No, that's not the only reason I'm here." He stepped closer. Her pulse raced at their proximity. "I'm really sorry about your mom. I should have been there for you." His eyes looked dark, heavy with remorse and sympathy.

"Oh, thanks, but I'm okay. Just need to take things one day at a time." She forced a smile.

"Look, I messed up. I'm an idiot for not calling you sooner. I haven't felt these feelings for someone in a long time, and the last time I did, my heart was broken."

She crossed her arms. "What about Sarah?"

He sighed. "She came to my office that day to tell me she'd made a mistake in letting me go. What you missed when you left was that I told her she had no chance. Nothing is going on or ever will be going on between Sarah and me again. Besides, I've fallen for someone else." He paused, waiting for Adrian to say something, but she stood there in silence. "If you'll let me," he continued, "I'd like to take you to dinner tomorrow night."

Adrian could barely hold back her smile. He was so adorably nervous, and it melted her heart. Her mother's words echoed in her mind: *A pair of twos is always worth betting on.* Was she ready to ante up?

Christian was worth the risk, and he was the only man she'd consider betting on. "It might take more than dinner." She smiled.

Relief spread over his face. "Good, because there's so much more I have planned than just dinner." He pulled her into his arms.

"Oh yeah, like what?"

"You'll have to wait and see," he whispered, and his lips touched hers. They stopped talking, getting lost in each other's embrace until they merged into one.

———

MARGARET WOULD HAVE APPROVED. They gathered in her honor on a Thursday evening at sunset on the beach, the sky painted with vibrant shades of pink and purple. The bright light of the sun illuminated the sky as it began its descent, ready to retire for the evening. The whole scene looked like it had been touched by Heaven, and perhaps in more than one way, Margaret was with them.

Adrian carried her in a vessel under her arm, her other hand using Christian as a crutch to steady her as they descended to the shore. Her long, violet halter dress rippled in the ocean breeze, hugging her silhouette. Christian looked like he'd emerged straight from a Tommy Bahama catalog in linen pants and a loose white shirt.

"Slow down," Gilda hollered behind them. She held a basket with a bottle of champagne and red plastic cups. She'd insisted on bringing the party, since Adrian wanted to carry the guest of honor.

"Don't worry, we'll catch up," Bev said, waving them on. Adrian looked over her shoulder to see the two of them using each other for support as they removed their sandals, toes digging in the sand. Gilda wore a navy sleeveless dress that grazed her knees, and Bev had on a cream cardigan over her brightly colored floral dress.

Harold was already playing footsie with the shoreline, his khaki pants rolled up to his calves while his sandals dangled off his fingertips. He looked out toward the horizon, and Adrian saw his mouth whispering something. She suspected he wanted a moment alone with her mother. Her heart ached for him.

"You want me to carry that?" Christian asked, referencing the container holding her mother's remains.

"She'd probably prefer that, but she's stuck with me." Adrian smiled, huddling closer to his arm.

As they approached Harold, she saw him wipe at the corner of his eye. Christian grabbed his shoulders and gave them a quick rub, and Harold smiled. They admired the beauty of the scene, waiting for Gilda and Bev to join.

"You sure it isn't too windy?" Bev held onto her knit hat. The wind *had* picked up a bit.

Christian licked his finger to gauge it. He nodded his head toward the west, indicating they should scatter her ashes in that direction to be safe. "I think we'll be good," he assured.

"Thank you all for coming this evening," Adrian said. "I wanted to do something nice to honor my mom with those closest to her. And to me." She looked at Christian. "I know she's looking down on us from above with a smile on her face." At that moment, the wind died down, and they smiled appreciatively at the Heavenly gesture.

Adrian handed the container to Harold. "Here, you should do the honors first." He tried to deny it, but she insisted. He held the container close, too choked up to say any words. Christian patted him on the back, and he found his strength again. He cracked the lid and exhaled, ready to scatter some of the remains in the ocean. An emotional lump formed in Adrian's throat, and Christian pulled her into his arms, intuitively knowing what she needed in that moment.

As Harold went to scatter some ashes, a gust of wind blew at the wrong time, Margaret scattering all over his face. He stood shell-shocked, his face covered in ash, while everyone else went slack-jawed.

"Oh, she's here alright." Gilda broke the silence. Bev chuckled, and they all laughed. Christian handed Harold a napkin from the basket, wiping his shoulders and chest to remove ashes.

"She always had a wicked sense of humor." Harold chuckled. Adrian realized even in death her mother could still surprise her.

"I think this calls for a toast," Christian said, and Gilda grabbed the champagne from the basket. He popped the cork, pouring a little into each cup as Gilda distributed them, Harold first.

"To Margaret," Gilda started, and they raised our cups. "May she rest in peace."

"That's it? So tame coming from you." Bev elbowed her.

"You think you can do better?" Gilda raised an eyebrow.

"Yeah, I think I can. To Margaret," Bev started, and they

raised their cups again. "A beautiful light that faded too soon but is shining brightly in Heaven."

"Uh-uh, no." Harold shook his head. "To Margaret," he started, and Adrian's arm felt tingly from holding it up in the air so long. "The best lover and friend a man could ask for." He gave a sly smile.

"You naughty boy." Gilda winked.

"Cheers!" Adrian said, and they all touched cups. The champagne tickled her tongue as it finally passed her lips.

"Think it's safe to scatter the rest?" Bev asked, looking at the sky for signs of wind.

Adrian looked at Christian, who licked his finger again to be sure. "Go for it," Christian said, pointing east.

Adrian handed the container to Gilda, and she held up her hand. "No, you should do it."

"You sure?" Gilda nodded. The wind nowhere to be found, Adrian opened the lid. *Goodbye, Ma.* She tipped the container, watching her mother's ashes fall into the ocean. They exploded like a mushroom cloud when they hit the water, and Adrian watched in awe as her mother merged with the waves. And just as quickly as they touched the water, her remains blended and disappeared in the wake. A single drop returning home to its true essence. Tears welled in Adrian's eyes.

Christian came up from behind, wrapping his arms around her. She squeezed his arm as he nuzzled her neck. "Think she'd approve of all this?"

She turned to kiss him. "Without a doubt."

EPILOGUE

Adrian dreamt of a night like this her entire life. Words failed to describe her excitement, and adrenaline-laced butterflies swarmed her body. The hum of idle chatter filled the Salt Grass Gallery as people imbibed and admired her highly anticipated collection. She still couldn't believe all those people had gathered in her honor.

She'd developed quite a name for herself in the art community in the panhandle. It didn't hurt that a lot of people knew and loved her father, but that night, she'd planned to officially step out from his shadow and stand alone in her talent. She'd bared her soul through a collection five years in the making: Portraits of Heaven.

Seeing her paintings contrasting the white walls in the gallery felt surreal. Nothing in the room could distract anyone from the beauty of the art she'd created. She never would have guessed that her life would have taken such a turn, but there she was, surrounded by love and art. How did she get so lucky?

She searched the room and saw Gilda's arm locked with Harold's, Bev following behind them as they admired one of her pieces. Harold and Gilda had become an item three years previously, and he'd agreed when Gilda said she and Bev were a packaged deal. "There's no way I'm leaving her singled out," she'd told Adrian at one of the poker nights they still held once a month. "She's my soulmate, Harold is just for fun." She'd winked. Bev continued the tradition of bringing baked goods to their monthly gatherings, and they both still cleaned Adrian out of nickels.

Christian held her hand as people congratulated her and praised her work. She fiddled nervously with the gold and diamond necklace around her neck. She'd had it made from her parents' wedding rings a few years back, and she never took it off. Christian squeezed her hand every time someone said kind words, a physical echo of agreement. She couldn't ask for a better partner, lover, and friend.

Christian and Adrian were married about six months after Margaret died. "When you know, you just know, and there's really no point in delaying," he'd said when he proposed to her in the same spot they'd scattered her mother's ashes. They held a small service on the beach at sunset, with a few close friends and relatives in attendance. Adrian knew her mother was present for the ceremony in spirit, nodding her head approvingly at Christian.

They were inseparable, their whirlwind romance consummating in a pregnancy shortly after their nuptials. She beat the odds when the doctor said her pregnancy was high-risk due to her previous injuries, and they'd welcomed a baby girl, Isabelle, with open arms. Parenting came naturally to both of them, bringing them closer together over the last five years.

The usual suspects from group therapy waved to them from across the room, although sadly, Henry wasn't in attendance. He'd died the previous year, finally reunited with his sweetheart in Heaven. Karen and Gina were standing next to the painting Adrian had made of Henry and Betty, giving her an enthusiastic thumbs up. Frank was arm in arm with his new partner, and Susan frantically chewed nicotine gum, having finally kicked the old habit. They still got together with each other once a month for old times' sake, although everyone had happily moved on with the next phases of their lives.

Laura and Zach approached them, looking impeccably sharp in a black satin knee-length sleeveless dress and matching wool suit. Laura had convinced Zach to move back to Pensacola. Thankfully, his employer had offered him a consulting role so he could work from home. At least she and Laura were only thirty minutes apart now. They'd always been inseparable, figuring out a way to stay together when life threw them curve balls over the years.

"Congrats, kid," Laura said, giving her a hug and a kiss on the cheek. She looked around the room approvingly. "I'd say this is your best work yet."

"Thanks, now why don't you show your appreciation with your wallet," Adrian joked, and they all laughed. Their attention moved to their children chasing each other through the gallery. She and Laura often mused about their kids being each other's best friends. "Maybe we'll be in-laws," Laura beamed when they joked about them getting married someday.

"Dylan, I told you not to run in here," she reminded him, catching him as they attempted to run past.

"Mommy, come quick," Isabelle insisted, pulling Adrian away from Christian.

"What is it, sweetheart?" she asked, as her daughter dragged her across the room, saying she needed to show her something. They stopped in front of the first painting in the collection, the one of the little girl on the other side.

"That's me, Mommy." Isabelle pointed at the portrait.

Adrian smiled. "Yes, it does look a lot like you."

"No, that's me," she insisted. "Look."

Adrian examined the portrait of the little girl she'd met on the other side years ago, the one who'd told her it wasn't her time yet and encouraged her to make things right with her mother. She looked into her daughter's eyes, realizing they were more familiar than she'd ever known. The honey ribbons woven throughout the hazel eyes, and her soft, pink, bow-shaped lips. There was no denying it. It was her, the little girl she'd met years ago, now standing in front of her. She couldn't speak, overwhelmed with emotion. How was that possible?

"You see now, don't you?" Isabelle smiled, twisting back and forth, her white and purple lace dress swishing from side to side.

"Yes." Tears welled in Adrian's eyes.

"She's okay too, you know." She pointed toward the picture of her and Margaret, the one Adrian had painted for her right before she died. Overcome with emotion, Adrian wiped her tear-stained cheeks.

"Don't cry, Mommy." Isabelle reached for her mother's hand, her tiny brow furrowed. "Be happy."

Adrian pulled her into a hug, gripping tightly. "I *am* happy, baby girl. More than you could ever know."

ACKNOWLEDGMENTS

Bringing this story to life was more challenging and rewarding than I ever imagined. Through its many different forms over many years, my parents, Linda Rash and Claude Hensley, were there every step of the way. I want to thank them for being my first fans from the moment I took my first breath. Thanks to Linda and Claude for being wonderfully supportive parents and encouraging my creativity. I couldn't have chosen better if I tried.

Also, I couldn't have done this without the support of my partner, Dwight Hume. Thank you, sweetheart, for allowing me to bend your ear about my story ad nauseum, for providing insight into the inner workings of the male brain, and for your love and encouragement. You continue to amaze me every day.

To the brave souls who read an early draft and helped shape the story into what it is today: Linda Rash, Claude Hensley, Mary Crockett, Eric Brown, Anita Hensley, Michelle Park, and Leigh Koritke; thank you, from the bottom of my heart. This book wouldn't exist without you.

To family and friends who are practically family: Pamella Hensley, Brette Rash, Jane Hume, Nina and Ligia

Miquel-Ghaziosharif, Lorie Vassar and Keena Jeffery; love you, and thank you for everything.

Behind every good story is hours of research, and this one is no different. Thank you, Paul A. Smith, for helping me understand the ins and outs of fertility and family law over shells of kava; Hemali Patel for answering medical questions; and Vivian Best for bravely sharing your experience with postpartum; without which the story would lack authenticity.

Thank you, Paula Lester, who polished my rough edges with her savvy edits, and Diren Yardimli for creating a work of art for the cover. Also, big thanks to Pat Dunlap Evans for developmental editing feedback that helped shape the story.

And most of all, thank you, Dear Reader, for spending time with the characters in this book. I sincerely hope you enjoyed them as much as I do.

ABOUT THE AUTHOR

Roxanne Hensley is the author of Women's Fiction and Romance with happily ever afters and a hint of magical realism. Always a storyteller, she earned a Bachelor's Degree in Creative Writing from Florida State University. When she's not writing, she spends her time reading one of the hundreds of books on her Kindle, shredding the air guitar, quoting movie lines and lyrics, crocheting, singing when she thinks no one is listening, or binge watching Netflix. She lives in Austin, Texas with her partner, Dwight, and two cats, Sookie and Gandalf.

To find out more about Roxanne and be the first to know about new releases, sign up for her newsletter on her official website: www.roxannehensley.com

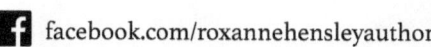 facebook.com/roxannehensleyauthor

 instagram.com/writerrox

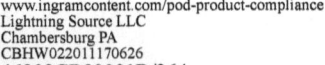